WILDFIRE

Suzanne Cass

S C
STORM CLOUD
PRESS

To my dad, he would've loved Montana

CHAPTER ONE

The deep-throated rumble of a motorcycle engine caught Levi Wilson's attention. He lifted his head and narrowed his eyes against the spring sunshine, trying to catch a glimpse of the bike on the winding road through the trees. It was coming fast, shiny black and silver chrome flashing in and out of the shadows.

Levi glanced back at the fallen tree blocking the road and walked up the white line along the tarmac, waving his arms to attract the rider's attention. How long was it going to take the town crew to get here? He'd been standing in the cold mountain air for over two hours, redirecting traffic back to the Pinetrail Road turnoff to avoid the large fir tree that'd come down in last night's storm. At least the tree hadn't downed any power lines, so the cleanup should be easy. Granted, this was a backroad, barely used except by locals wanting to avoid the main highway into Stevensville, and he'd only seen three vehicles so far. But he had a lot to do today and standing guard on a backwater road into the valley had *not* been on his list.

The roar got louder as the motorcycle swung around the last bend and accelerated straight towards him. Was this rider crazy? They were treating the winding country road like a racetrack.

Levi waved his arms wildly, jogging up the road. He had to stop this madman before he rode directly into the tree. Couldn't he see the large trunk lying diagonally across the road, broken limbs sticking up at odd angles toward the sky? The motorcycle kept coming, and Levi was about to step off the road before he got hit, when the rider finally applied the brakes.

The motorcycle came to a smooth stop only five feet in front of Levi, the rider planting their feet to steady the large bike. Wearing black leathers and a black, full-face helmet, the rider sat completely still, silently watching Levi. Who the hell did this guy think he was? He probably thought it was funny, trying to scare a park ranger by driving straight at him. And then trying to psych him out with the sinister, black outfit. Levi didn't care if this guy was the leader of the Hells Angels, he was about to hear exactly what Levi thought…

Hang on. That motorcycle looked familiar. His gaze raked over the shiny, black gas tank and fenders. It was a big touring bike. A Triumph. Now he was up close, he could see the rider was lithe and slender, too small to be a man.

Levi's blood ran cold, and a tight knot formed in the pit of his stomach.

It couldn't be.

He stood there in the middle of the road, staring at the leather-clad rider on the large bike as if frozen to the spot. No words would come, his brain was numb with shock.

The rider shrugged and then lifted their hands, slowly removing the helmet.

It was her. She was back.

His heart beat wildly in his chest.

"Levi," she said, her tone soft in the cold, morning air.

He finally found his voice. "Cat Lawson." His gaze hungrily searched her face. Those blue eyes, like he was looking at a perfect piece of Montana summer sky. Hair still short and blonde, almost boyish, spiked at the top like a rock star, longer fringe hanging in her eyes. The eyebrow stud was still there, as were the numerous ear piercings. It'd been six months since he'd seen her, but everything about her was still etched, crystal-clear into his mind's eye. He used to think it was the face of an angel.

"What are you doing here?"

She lowered her eyes, seeming to find something interesting on the toe of her biker boot. "Dean called me. Wants me back at Stargazer Ranch. Something about their last mechanic being a complete dick, and that no one can fix a snowmobile like I can." She glanced up and her lips twitched, as if she were about to smile.

Levi remembered that smile, the one that had a gravitational pull, luring him in, like he was the earth orbiting the sun. He wasn't going to be taken in this time, however.

"I was going to tell you. Once I got settled—"

"Bullshit!" His loud exclamation made her lift her head sharply, finally locking gazes with him.

"Look, I'm sorry, Levi. I really am."

He doubted it. After the callous way she left, not even able to tell him to his face that she was leaving.

"But…"

Here it came, the excuse he'd been waiting for.

"We were never going to make it together, not really. I did us a favor when I moved on."

They'd only been together for a month. Not nearly long enough for him to fall in love with her. Or so everyone kept telling him. Probably in an effort to make him feel better. He'd hidden his devastation behind a smile and a wave.

"I promise to stay out of your way," she said, slipping the helmet back over her head, hiding her blue eyes once more.

"Take the first road on the left, about half a mile back," he replied, voice deadpan, finger pointing up the road. "Pinetrail Road, then take the first left again into Wildfowl Lane, and that'll take you into the back end of Stevensville, past…" He was about to say *my office* but changed his mind. "…the district ranger's office." He was here to do a job. Direct people around the fallen tree until the cleanup crew got here. No special favors for a girl he used to know.

Cat started the motorcycle, and a raspy grumble filled the air. Cat had once told him she loved that bike more than anything else in the world. Because it gave her freedom. Back when they'd been dating, he'd thought to replace that bike in her heart. But she'd been right all along. The bike meant more to her than any human. She wasn't meant for love. Or at least, not meant for love with him.

She skillfully maneuvered the bike, so it faced away from him and then took off with a spurt of speed, not looking back. Not even once. Levi pulled the government-issue park ranger jacket tighter around him, reaching for the zipper. Stamping his boots on the tarmac, he tried to get some circulation back into his toes. It was suddenly so cold, standing alone in the middle of the road, the shadows of the forest trees crowding in around him.

Where the hell was that town cleanup crew? He went back to his ranger truck, parked on the side of the road near the tree, and unhooked his hand-held radio. They needed to get their butts up here quick-smart; he was tired of waiting. After talking into his radio for a few minutes, letting them know in no uncertain terms he wasn't happy, he sat in the front seat of his car and glared at the road up which Cat had just disappeared.

He remembered the first time he'd ever set eyes on Cat; he'd had to rescue her from a burning cabin over at Stargazer Ranch, lit by an arsonist targeting the owners. Even though she'd determinedly denied she needed rescuing.

But then, less than a week later, she'd rescued him right back, when his house had been set on fire by the very same arsonist. Even in that short week, passion had sparked bright and hot between them. Cat was skittish and unpredictable. Believed she was a free spirit, who didn't need anyone or anything. Perhaps he should've listened to the alarm bells ringing then. But like an idiot, he'd dived headfirst into a relationship with her. And look where that'd got him.

His mind wandered back to Cat sitting astride her Triumph, the black leathers hugging her body like a second skin. She was so damn sexy. Tattoos covering each arm. And she must have at least a dozen silver studs in each ear. On most women, they would've been a turn-off for him. But not on Cat. Levi remembered the taste of her skin on his tongue. How she used to arch her long neck so that he could fan kisses all the way down from her earlobe to her collarbone. He also remembered how she used her tattoos and tough persona as a coat of armor, to hide the real Cat from the world.

What the hell did he think he was doing? They were two people who were so different, it wasn't funny. They wanted the complete opposite in life. He got out of the car and slammed the door. Then stomped impatiently down the road to wait for the town crew to arrive and clean up this shitty mess.

CHAPTER TWO

Cat cursed loudly inside her helmet. Of all the people she could've run into on her first day back in the valley. Of course, it had to be Levi. She slowed the motorcycle to take a sharp bend leading into the main street of Stevensville. It was Saturday morning and the street was busy. Trucks and SUVs lined the streets, parked in the angled bays along the curb. People ambled along the sidewalks, and cafe tables spilled out onto the street, full of happy diners. The sight of the quaint shops fringing the street tickled her memory. It was almost like coming home again.

The thought brought her up abruptly. Should she just keep going? Take off down the road? Let the powerful motor carry her away to someplace there were no complications? She hadn't promised Dean anything over the phone when he called a week ago. Said she'd think about it, that was all. But even before she ended the call, she knew she'd return.

Something about this place, the Bitterroot Valley snuggled in the foothills of the Bitterroot Mountains, Montana called to her. The beauty up here made her heart ache. Green pine trees marched up to the imposing silhouette of St. Mary Peak, the highest mountain in the area, so stark and barren. Today, its head was covered in spring snow. The freezing water of the

Bitterroot River, clear and pure, rippled over the stones. It was simply stunning; how could anyone not be affected?

She'd worked at Stargazer for nearly a year, and in that time the peace had begun to pierce her soul. It was the longest she'd ever stayed in one place. Cat had almost convinced herself she might even stay forever. Then she'd met Levi. And for a month, life had been almost perfect. Except for that insidious little voice inside her head telling her to run before it was too late. She'd allowed Levi's soft caresses and the way he looked at her, like she was someone special, to seep through her defenses. She'd given in to weakness and let herself fall for him. She told herself it hadn't been love. It was lust, pure and simple, but even then, in the end, it'd become too complicated. Cat wasn't cut out for commitment. And Levi deserved more. Her heart had frozen over years ago, and she was better off on her own. Freedom was all that mattered.

She'd only come back for one reason—because Dean needed her. Okay, maybe two reasons. Because this small, country town and Dean's luxury ranch had wormed their way deep inside her chest, leaving a longing that she hoped to rid herself of by another visit. She'd stay and help Dean over the summer, then move on. That was the way she always lived. Moving from one place to the next. There was so much to see, so much to do in this life, she couldn't possibly be tied down to one place. Not forever, anyway.

Cat cleared the outskirts of town and opened up the throttle, letting the bike take her south down the highway, almost as if it knew the way without her guidance, like a horse finding its way back to a stable.

Her mind wandered to Levi, how he'd looked standing in the middle of the road, hands up, demanding she halt. It'd taken her a few seconds to recognize him. It wasn't until she came to a complete stop in front of him that her blood fired hot through her veins, as if her soul acknowledged his presence, even before her brain did.

Perhaps it was because Levi now sported a beard. It was short, neatly trimmed, but gave him even more of a mountain-man appearance. It suited him. He'd always had at least a three-day growth when they'd dated, which gave him that rugged appeal. But the beard was perhaps even better. At least he still had his long, dark hair, tied back at the nape of his neck. It would be sacrilege if he ever cut that off.

The second he turned those earth-colored eyes on her, her body reacted. At least her small gasp of shock had been hidden behind her visor. She'd taken those few seconds of grace, while she removed her helmet, to re-center herself, recompose her face into lines of disinterest. Of course, she'd known she might come in contact with Levi on her return to Stevensville, but she'd hoped for a few days, weeks even, to prepare. As it was, she congratulated herself on keeping her face cool and blank, not giving away the turmoil grinding in her guts.

Maybe it was a good thing. At least their first meeting was over. He knew she was back, and hopefully she'd given him enough so he wouldn't come prying for answers and leave her alone.

Almost on autopilot, Cat slowed the big motorcycle as she crested a hill and the large, stone wall marking the entrance to Stargazer Ranch appeared over the rise. Guiding her bike smoothly onto the dirt, she flipped open her visor and drew in a deep breath of clean, mountain air. Soon, individual log cabins were slipping past on either side as she wound her way into the foothills. Dean had built twenty luxury cabins on the property, all completely secluded, just the way the guests liked it. People came all year round to partake in the many activities the resort offered, like horseback riding or hiking in the summer, or skiing and dog sledding in the winter.

A few smaller roads branched off the main drive, heading deeper into the pines, where more cabins were hidden. Before she knew it, Cat had threaded her way through a tunnel of overhanging branches and emerged into a huge, open area of rolling hills and fields. And there, nestled into a valley, sat the main lodge. It'd once been a large, old, log farmhouse, built by the first owners of this property. The guy had big dreams, but he'd run out of money before he got to finish the house. When Dean and Naomi bought it fifteen years before, it had good bones, with soaring ceilings and lots of large windows to take in the views; it just needed some remodeling, and a whole lot of TLC. Now, it was so beautiful it nearly took Cat's breath away. It could almost be called a log mansion. It rambled across the hillside over three levels. The main level was held up by many sturdy, wooden poles, supporting a large, open decking that ran all the way around, allowing the ultimate vista of the surrounding mountains. This level contained the communal area, with a huge, five-star restaurant and a vaulted foyer ceiling that opened up to large windows at the top to show off the big, never-ending sky. There was an open-plan reception area, and lots of big and small sitting rooms scattered throughout for guests to gather in, as well as the kitchen out back, where the staff would often come together for a communal meal. Two wings fanned out on either side of the main building, housing ten luxury rooms for people who wanted the lodge experience but didn't need a whole cabin to themselves. Dean and Naomi had private quarters nestled at the top of the building, on the second level. From her position in the front parking lot, she could see the undercover area at ground level, which was where the weekly barbecues were held. People could play Ping-Pong, or darts, and gather beside the large, open-pit fireplace. Half a dozen or so people milled around the main reception area now, probably guests getting ready to check out. Naomi would be busy making sure everyone had an enjoyable stay. And Dean would probably be playing the gregarious host. He loved to talk. He was good at using his southern charm to captivate his guests, and they all left feeling as if they were somehow special. Which they were, in Dean's eyes. He wanted to make sure every single person who visited his ranch had a great time. Dean was also part-owner of another luxury ranch in Australia that was run by his sister and her husband. Cat dreamed of visiting Stormcloud Station one day. She'd never been to tropical North Queensland, but it was on her bucket list.

It wasn't the best time to be announcing her arrival. A large stable, along with the horse paddocks, was partially hidden to the left and behind the lodge. Two palomino faces hung over the corner fence. She decided to head down there, instead, and come back when the rush of checkout had finished. Propping her bike on its kickstand, she removed her helmet and stretched her tired legs as she dismounted. It'd been a long ride; she'd started out at six a.m. and had ridden straight through for over six hours.

A loud, tuneless whistle filled the air as Cat rounded the side of the lodge and made her way toward the stable. There was only one person who could whistle that loud. Big Tom had his back to her, fiddling with a saddle set up on the top rail of one of the horse stalls. She knew it was him, even without his trademark red-plaid shirt and buckskin-colored cattleman's hat, because he was so goddamned tall. Her bicycle boots made hardly any sound on the dry sawdust covering the floor as she crept into the stables. She managed to get within a few feet of him, when a horse a few stalls down gave a low whicker of greeting. Big Tom spun around and released a gush of air when he saw who it was.

"Jesus, Cat. Scare a man half to death, you would."

She grinned and then punched him in the shoulder. "You should stop whistling so loud, then you might hear people coming."

But he wasn't letting her get away that easily. "Come here." He gathered her in his arms and squeezed her so tight all the air left her lungs. Then he planted her firmly on the ground and leaned against the saddle he'd been fixing. "Welcome back. Dean told us you might turn up."

Big Tom had always been one of her favorites. "Thanks," she said, warmth tightening her chest. "It's good to be back." The words surprised her, but it was the truth. The smell of the stables was cozy and familiar. Cat walked over to stroke the nose of the horse who'd given her away. He was a gorgeous dark chestnut, with a white star on his forehead. Cat racked her brain, and finally remembered the horse's name. Star. Of course. He closed his eyes in satisfaction as she scratched the spot between his ears. Emily and Tom had taught her to ride last time she was here, and she did okay in the saddle. But give her a motorcycle any day to make her truly happy.

"How's Emily?" she asked.

"Glad to hear she's getting her roomie back."

"Cool." Cat kept her reply light, but secretly, she was delighted to hear she'd be rooming with Emily again in the little cottage up the hill from the lodge. They'd become firm friends last year, but Cat had been worried that leaving in such a hurry six months ago might've put a dent in their friendship. This sounded promising.

"You're looking good," Tom said, glancing appreciatively at her tight, black leathers. Normally, Cat would shut down any kind of flirtatious behavior with a co-worker, but she knew Tom meant no harm; they were friends, nothing more. "Be better when you're back into jeans and plaid, though." He winked and Cat rolled her eyes.

"What you been up to for the last few months?" Tom

asked, staring at her with unnerving intent.

"Oh, you know, this and that." Cat kept her focus firmly fixed on the horse. She wasn't being intentionally vague. Jobs weren't usually difficult to find. Her mechanical skills were top-notch. At least she could thank her father for that. Even if it was the only good thing she ever got from him. And once she got past the usual stereotypical discrimination because she was a woman, most garages were glad to have her.

"I drove down to Las Vegas. Found a job with a Cadillac limo rental company. Even got to meet some celebrities," she said, squaring her shoulders and finally looking him in the eye.

But he just smiled. "Wow, girl, you really wanted to get as far away from here as possible, didn't you?"

She hunched her shoulders and glared at him. That hadn't been it, at all. She'd always wanted to see Las Vegas, and when she left Stargazer, it'd seemed like the perfect time to go. She decided not to tell him that she'd ridden the nine-hundred odd miles to Las Vegas in one go. Hightailed it right through the night, only stopping to refuel on caffeine, or for a bathroom break. Because then he might get really smug.

Before he could delve further into the subject of why she thought she had to run away—and perhaps bring up the subject of Levi—she went on, "It was a great job. And Las Vegas truly is everything they say, and more."

"Yeah, I can imagine," Tom drawled with a wry twist to his mouth.

She was beginning to wonder why on earth she'd decided to come back and how she could have possibly thought the people here were nicer than anywhere else.

"Anyway," she continued with a huff, "I was headed to Flagstaff when Dean called. Thought I might go and see the Grand Canyon."

"It is beautiful down there." Tom's eyes got a faraway look.

But Cat didn't want to get sidetracked by Arizona, or the Grand Canyon. She had one question that'd been burning like a brand in her mind, ever since she'd decided to come back. "Has anyone seen Clayton?"

Big Tom shook his head. "Nope. And we all hope to keep it that way. There haven't been any fires since he disappeared, either."

"What about the cops? Have they got any leads? Any idea where he is?" Clayton had been a ranch hand at Stargazer. He'd also been responsible for setting three fires on the ranch last year. And he'd almost managed to kill Levi by setting fire to his house, as well. If Cat hadn't been there, hadn't dived into his burning house to save him, Levi might well have died. Been burned alive. She broke out in a fine sweat at the thought.

It was a little ironic, really. The first time she'd met Levi, he'd run into a burning cabin to find her, after she went in to rescue a guest's dog. Then, less than a week later, she'd returned the favor by pulling him out of his own house, set alight by the same arsonist, Clayton.

Clayton's pickup had been found crashed and abandoned a few miles from Levi's house on the same night as the fire. And Levi had been sure it was Clayton he'd seen right before he'd been hit over the head, although he admitted later, his memory was a little foggy. The cops had been looking for Clayton ever since. Cat had hoped they'd caught up with him by now. But it sounded like he was still on the run.

"No, they say they're still following up on some leads. But we all know what that means." Tom scowled. "It means they couldn't find their own asshole with a flashlight and a map."

Cat couldn't help it, she let out a loud guffaw. Tom always did have a way with words.

"I just hope he stays the hell away from here," Tom said, fists clenched at his side. Cat knew what he meant, because she felt the same way. If she ever saw Clayton again… All number of things she might do to him flashed through her head. He just better not show his face, that was all.

"What about that email Dean got? When the fires started? Has he had any more of those?" Cat asked.

"Nope. Not to my knowledge. And you know Dean likes to stay as transparent as possible."

Cat pursed her lips in agreement. Back when the fires had first begun, Dean had let his staff know that someone had sent him a threatening email. He'd made sure they all felt safe, kept them working in pairs, and said that if any of them wanted to leave, he'd give them a nice bonus. The cops never found out who sent Dean the threat, but once Clayton had been named as the arsonist, everyone assumed it was him.

"The Applegate's came back," Tom said, leaning against the railing. "They were here a few weeks ago, with their dog. Remember him? What was he called? Jasper, or something like that?"

Oh yes, she remembered Jasper, all right. She'd risked her life to rescue that damn dog from the burning log cabin. "That's great. At least they're not harboring any grudges or blaming Dean for what happened." Which was good. The Applegate's were one of Dean's oldest guests, they'd been coming here ever since the luxury ranch opened, fifteen years ago. They were both well into their seventies, but still loved to hike and horse ride whenever they visited the ranch.

"Nope. Old Frank told Dean that no arsonist was going to scare him away from his favorite vacation spot in the whole world." Tom laughed. Then he sobered. "I think Pamela needed a bit of convincing, however."

Cat could imagine the tough old man pursing his lips and lowering his enormous eyebrows as he defied the danger. She wasn't surprised that Pamela was more hesitant, however. She'd been almost hysterical at the time of the fire and had sobbed and sobbed into her Pomeranian's fur after Cat rescued him. It would've been a shock for anyone. Cat just wished they knew more about the arsonist. Why they were targeting the ranch; what their intentions were.

"Has Dean rebuilt the cabin yet?"

"No." Tom gave a despondent smile. "The insurance company took a while to come through. And Dean keeps coming up with excuses…you know." Tom shrugged, and Cat understood what he was implying. Dean was hesitant to rebuild because he was superstitious. Didn't want to bring any more bad luck down on the ranch. She understood his reluctance, even if she didn't agree with it.

Tom spent the next fifteen minutes catching Cat up on what the other staff had been up to. Everyone else was pretty much still here, except for Talia, the chef's apprentice, who'd left to pursue a career in a big restaurant in Los Angeles. A new girl, Stella, had replaced her, and according to Tom, she had all the single boys on the ranch eating out of her hand. She was French and gorgeous, an irresistible mixture, supposedly. He mentioned the mechanic, Preston, who'd been hired to replace Cat when she left without warning. Preston had ended up getting on the wrong side of Dean. Tom didn't know exactly what'd happened; all he knew was they had a disagreement, and tensions remained high. Then a few weeks later, Preston announced he got a better job in town. Tom found it a little ironic that Preston had gone the same day Dean phoned Cat to offer her job back. Perhaps he caught wind that Dean was going to replace him and jumped before he was pushed.

Cat gave a dry smile and left Tom to get back to his saddle repairs. It was time to go and say hello to Dean and Naomi. To change out of her leathers and back into her *jeans and plaid*, as Tom put it. Slip back into ranch life, like she'd never left.

CHAPTER THREE

Levi let his hand rest on the door handle of his truck. He drew in a deep breath and let it out again. He could do this. The unexpected meeting with Cat yesterday—he'd been caught off guard and unaware—had rattled him. But he was prepared, this time. If he ran into her today, he would be cool, polite, and self-possessed.

Taking one more deep breath, Levi pushed on the handle and opened his truck door, stepping down onto the gravel parking lot out front of Stargazer Lodge. A blast of cold air tried to claw its way through his jacket. It might be spring, but in the Montana mountains, that could still mean temperatures close to freezing. He fished his park-issue knit cap out of his jacket pocket and pulled it down over his ears.

Dean had asked to meet him at the lodge, so he could show him some maps of the property, before Levi went out on his mission. As Levi made his way up the wooden walkway leading him through a wild-looking, cottage-style garden, and over a small bridge crossing a burbling stream, he took in the large lodge. It was a beautiful bit of log-cabin craftsmanship. Dean and Naomi had done a wonderful job of making this place their home, and turning it into one of the best boutique, luxury resorts in the whole Rocky Mountain

Range.

Taking the steps up to the deck two at a time, Levi looked up to see Dean waiting at the top, holding the large, glass door open for him. Levi knew the man was in his late fifties, but he sure didn't look it in his plaid shirt, sheepskin vest, and blue jeans, tall and strong and commanding. The light sprinkle of grey at his temples, in contrast to his dark hair, might give him away. But his face was warm and welcoming, almost childlike, it was so alive with humor and excitement. Levi liked Dean. He and his wife were so down-to-earth and personable. They didn't act like billionaires. Well, not in the way Levi thought a billionaire might act.

"Thanks for coming at such short notice," Dean said, offering his hand. Levi shook it and went into the welcome warmth of the reception area. In the seven months Levi had been working as the park ranger in the area, he'd been to Stargazer Ranch at least a dozen times. Dean had been forever thankful to him for rescuing Cat from the burning cabin on his very first week on the job, and made sure Levi knew he was welcome whenever he wanted to come. Naomi had even invited him to share dinner with them and the staff a few times. But after Cat had left—dumped him—Levi found it awkward, and so tended to only come on official business.

Which was exactly why he was there today. He really hoped he could keep Dean away from the subject of Cat's return. But he steeled himself for the inevitable questions.

"Come into my office." Dean strode in front of Levi, leading the way to a room right behind the grand reception area. Every time Levi visited, he couldn't help but marvel at the front desk, made of one huge piece of pine, cut from a tree hundreds of years old, right here on the property. He smiled at Penny, who stood on duty, waiting to help the guests. She was pretty and she gave him a flirty smile in return.

Levi removed his knit cap and coat as Dean closed the door behind them and waved Levi over to his desk. It was also solid pine, and completely cluttered with maps spread over the surface. Some of the maps looked really old, and Levi was drawn in, leaning down to take a look. They were all of the ranch and the surrounding mountains.

"I found these up in the attic last night, after I called you," Dean said. "The previous owner must've stashed them up there. I love how I keep finding stuff I never knew existed." Dean gave his trademark beaming smile, as if he'd found a pot of gold, instead of some old maps. "Here's a couple of newer topographic ones, too." He lifted a few sheets and pulled out the modern maps. They'd be more useful for the mission Levi was going to undertake today. They'd give him more information on the lay of the land, the ridges and valleys, streams and high, rocky outcrops he might have to traverse. Along with any trails marked in the wilderness.

"I looked on Google Maps last night," Levi said, stroking his beard as he stared down at the map. He'd started growing it after Cat left. Probably as an act of defiance, if he were to attempt to self-analyze his behavior. But also, just to see if he could. A lot of Native American men found it hard to grow a beard, and most of them remained clean-shaven. Because of his mother's Italian heritage, he'd been blessed with hairy genes, and he was making damn good use of them.

"But I know reception is pretty patchy up there," he continued, "so I won't be able to rely on it for today. These will help, thanks."

"We think it might be hiding out in this valley, right here." Dean placed a finger on the map, pointing at a spot up on the slopes of Downing Mountain, about a mile away from the main lodge.

Levi leaned closer and peered at the markings on the map. "It looks pretty rough, and here's a ravine heading off the valley. Probably a few caves and crevices up there for it to hide in."

"That's what we decided, too." Dean nodded thoughtfully. "But it's still close enough for that beast to come down every night to conduct his raids."

"Hmm," Levi replied, still lost in the hills and valleys on the map, trying to plan the best route to take.

Dean had called him the previous night, saying the ranch had a rogue grizzly on their hands. Grizzly bears were rare in this part of the Rockies, but every now and then, one was spotted. It was mainly the smaller black bears found everywhere. This grizzly, however, was making a nuisance of itself, raiding the large chicken coop and the feed shed. At first the incidents were infrequent, but lately he'd been coming every night, now even trying to get into the bear-proof bins at the back of the property. It was getting so that Dean was worried about his guests' safety, as they walked between the lodge and their individual cabins to take in the famous starry sky after dinner. Levi suspected the bear might be injured, or old, which was why his raids had increased. No matter the reason, the bear needed to be traced, and a plan formulated to relocate him. It was Levi's job to look for him, then call in more help if needed.

"This one must've come out of hibernation early," Levi mused, almost to himself. This spring was milder than normal, and Levi had already spotted a couple of black bears roaming around.

"Yes, it's the warm weather waking them up," Dean said.

Which almost made Levi laugh. Most people wouldn't call it *warm* here in spring. But he knew what Dean meant. The winter hadn't been as bitterly cold this year, and the snow melt had started nearly a month before it normally would.

Dean took two strides over to the side table running the length of one wall of the office. "Can I get you a coffee?"

There was a coffee pot on the table, as well as a stack of mugs, and all the makings for tea, coffee, or hot chocolate.

"That'd be great, thanks." Levi had been going since five a.m. and although he'd gulped down breakfast on his way out of the house, a hot cup of pick-me-up would be most welcome. "With half-and-half, if you've got it, please." Levi hadn't slept well last night, which was partly the reason he was up so early this morning. Images of Cat, astride her motorcycle, blue eyes blazing in the morning sunshine, had dogged him all night, no matter how he tried to rid himself of them. After she'd left the previous day, the town crew had taken another two hours to arrive and begin cleaning up the fallen tree. Which had given Levi plenty of time to ruminate on her return.

The other reason he'd been up so early had to do with a certain little critter. Rekker was screaming so loud to be let inside, Levi thought he might wake the neighbors. He'd found the injured adolescent raccoon in his back yard a few months ago. He'd taken him to the vet, and then applied for a permit to become a wildlife rehabilitator, and the young raccoon had moved in with him. It wasn't recommended for people to keep raccoons as a pet, but Levi had no choice; the little guy would've died without him. It hadn't taken long for Levi to come up with the name Rekker. Because that seemed to be the young animal's main aim in life. To destroy everything he got his little paws on. They weren't called the master of thieves for no reason. But Rekker was also adorable and had burrowed a deep place in Levi's heart. During the day Rekker was free to roam around outside—or inside, if Levi was home—but at night he was locked in a raccoon-friendly compound he'd built for his critter companion in the back yard. Rekker didn't like being cooped up—especially at night, as he was nocturnal—and he let Levi, and the rest of the world, know about it.

Dean handed Levi a mug, and they both sipped on the rejuvenating liquid in silence. Dean glanced up and something flashed in the older man's eyes that made Levi feel suddenly uncomfortable. He was going to bring up the subject of Cat, he just knew it. He didn't need any questions, no matter how well-meaning, on how he felt about Cat being back in town.

He gulped the hot liquid, burning his tongue, then placed the cup quickly down on the desk. "I'll go and get started. My truck should be able to get at least partway up that trail marked on the map. I can walk the rest of the way." He started to pull on his coat, heading for the door.

"Hold your horses." Dean's voice stopped him in his tracks. He was folding up one of the maps, presumably for Levi to take with him. "You know we have a fleet of four-wheelers, don't you?"

Levi had forgotten, but now that Dean mentioned it, he remembered Cat repairing one when he'd visited the ranch before.

"Those four-wheelers can get into terrain that your truck wouldn't handle." Dean stared at Levi, a strange gleam in his eye that Levi couldn't decipher. "I've arranged for you to borrow one; it'll get you much closer to that ravine." Dean handed him the map.

"Oh." Levi stopped moving. "Okay, that would be helpful. Thanks."

"Come on, I'll take you up to the machinery workshop." Dean grabbed a coat from a hook on the back of his door and walked out. It was a heavy, brown overcoat, emblazoned with the Stargazer Ranch emblem on the back. All the staff were given one to wear. Levi remembered Cat only used to wear hers begrudgingly; she hated to conform to anything. Then it hit him—Cat might well be working at the machinery shed. There was a slight possibility she wouldn't be there, but she was the ranch mechanic, and even if this was her first day back on the ranch, that was where she loved to be.

He glowered at Dean's back. The man had set him up. He'd known all along how this was going to go down.

Levi drove his truck up to the workshop, Dean riding shotgun. It took a moment for Levi to readjust to the crisp air, after the warmth of the centrally-heated lodge. This was a large ranch, and even the outbuildings were a fair walk from the main hub. Dean and Naomi supplied specially altered electric golf carts to the guests to get around on the winding maze of roads that crisscrossed the ranch. The carts were modified so they could handle the deep snow that sometimes blanketed the ranch in winter. Some guests liked to walk, to take in the beautiful, unending vistas, breathe in the clear air, and get the heart pumping. After all, most of the guests were here to partake in the physical activities offered at the resort, like hiking and horse riding. But some of them were elderly or preferred the ease of driving.

They pulled up outside the machinery workshop—which was actually a really large barn, where all the four-wheelers, snowmobiles, golf carts, ranch vehicles and even some of the ranch machinery were kept.

As he brought his truck to a stop, Levi pondered the best way to get up to the mountain, to keep his mind off the possibility of seeing Cat again. Even though Dean owned all the land up to the first ridgeline of the Bitterroot Mountains, there were fences lining the boundaries of Dean's pastures that'd need to be negotiated.

Levi gathered his backpack, which was filled with equipment and food that he'd need to take with him, out of the rear seat of his truck, and followed Dean inside the large, red building. The interior was enormous, the ceiling soaring two stories above their heads, and Levi wrinkled his nose at the smell of dust and grease. It was bright in here, large rows of windows up high letting in lots of natural light. Levi already knew the layout of the building; he'd visited Cat here a few times back when… He shut that thought down quickly.

All the four-wheelers were parked neatly in rows on the left-hand side. Behind them, the snowmobiles were also lined up, covered with tarpaulins, now that winter was over. All types of machinery in need of repair filled the other side of the shed, with the area in between left open and clear. A spot at the far end was lit up, a huge workbench covered in tools, and a circle of grease-spotted concrete singled out the main work area.

Levi stopped in front of the first four-wheeler expectantly, but Dean kept walking toward the back.

Suddenly a voice fractured the silence in the barn. "That mechanic guy you hired was a slob. Look at these tools. He's put them away dirty—when he even bothered to put them away at all—and he's left the place looking like a pigsty."

Levi's head jerked up, and he stared down the long hallway towards the workbench at the rear.

"That's why I needed you back, Cat," Dean said.

Oh. Shit. Levi quashed the urge to turn on his heel and walk out. He was an adult. He could do this. Be polite and professional.

Cat had her back to Dean, rummaging through something on the workbench. But Levi could tell the exact moment she spotted him as she turned around. Her eyes widened, and then just as quickly narrowed. She halted in her tracks, wrench in her hand stalled half-way off the bench.

"Look who I brought. He needs to borrow a four-wheeler." Dean beamed at Cat like he was bringing her the best surprise in the world.

CHAPTER FOUR

"What the hell is he doing here?" The words left her lips before she could stop them. Dean should've warned her he was bringing Levi. He knew their history. She glared at Dean, but he gave her that ingratiating grin he used to disarm all his foes.

"Nice to see you, too, Cat."

Cat didn't deign to reply. Dean had set her up. Because, of course, Dean knew she'd be here. They'd discussed what he needed from her last night over the dinner table. She'd told him she couldn't wait to get started again. It'd been nice, sitting with all the other staff, eating and talking like she'd never even left. But it seemed like Dean might've been softening her up. Cat gave a snort of derision and decided the best course of action was to ignore them both. She turned her back and pretended to be rummaging through the toolbox again.

"Levi is going up into the foothills of Downing Peak, and he needs a quad," Dean said chirpily.

Cat waved a hand in the general direction of the vehicles. "He can take whichever one he likes from the front row; they should all work fine." Which might not be strictly true, because she hadn't had a chance to check them all yet, but as long as the other mechanic had followed protocol, all the ones needing repairs would be parked at the back, out of reach. She didn't turn around as she spoke.

"He's going out to check on the visitor I told you about last night. That grizzly who's been using the ranch as his own personal lunchbox." Dean continued in the way-too-chirpy tone that was beginning to annoy Cat. She lifted one shoulder. Why should she care what Levi was up to?

"And I don't want him going on his own, so I thought you could accompany him."

She stilled. What had Dean just said?

"You never mentioned any of this last night." Cat turned and put her hands on her hips, throwing an accusing look at Dean. If he hadn't been her boss, she might well have told him where he could go. There was no way she was going anywhere with Levi. Not today. Not any day.

"I don't need any help, thanks anyway, Dean," Levi said from his spot near the four-wheeler. Cat glanced in his direction, noting his raised eyebrow. A sign that meant he was just as incredulous as she was. Levi wasn't in on this plan, then. It was all Dean. She turned to glare at her boss.

He met her gaze with his own level stare. "I don't want Levi going up there alone. What if the grizzly takes a dislike to him and charges? Or if he gets lost or hurt?"

"I've got a sat phone, I'll be fine. Besides—"

Dean held up a hand to stop Levi's exclamation.

"You know we've had a rule about working alone, ever since those fires last year." Dean's voice was calm, but she could hear the steel running through his tone. He meant what he said. And he wasn't going to take no for an answer.

She wanted to say that Levi wasn't a Stargazer staff member, but even she knew that'd sound petty. Dean had a valid point. But why did it have to be her?

As if reading her mind, Dean said, "Tom is busy with the

blacksmith today, and Emily and Steph are out on a cattle drive with some of the guests. So no, they can't do it."

She wanted to ask about Dean's nephew, Dale? He was another cowboy on the ranch, sent over for training from their sister property in Australia. Or even Gordon, the activities manager. But she managed to stop herself, grinding her teeth together instead. Dean was her boss. And even though she'd like to argue the point with him, she knew by the look in his eye that Dean would only be pushed so far today. She'd just got back; she didn't want to be turfed off the ranch for being insubordinate on her first day. It wouldn't be the first time she'd been fired because of her sharp tongue. Because she liked to defy authority. But today, she wanted to keep her job.

Cat glanced back at Levi, who hadn't said anything more, merely watched their exchange. A deep frown furrowed his high forehead, and the beard that she was still getting used to bristled as he pursed his lips. It looked like he was equally unhappy about this turn of events. Actually, he looked downright pissed off.

His frown was so deep, it became painfully obvious that Levi *really* didn't want her to go. Something twinged inside Cat's chest. Which was stupid. Because she *really* didn't want to go, either. So, why would it hurt that he was rejecting her?

Cat let out an exasperated groan. This was the reason she stayed away from love. Why she'd run away from him in the first place. It was all too complicated and hard to work out. Everything was easier if you only had yourself to look after. It was one of the reasons she loved her motorcycle so much; it never talked back.

"Fine. I'll need to go get some gear. Give me ten minutes."

"Thank you, Cat." Dean was all cheerful smiles again. The traitor.

"I've got plenty of food and water," Levi said, as she strode past him and out the large workshop door.

"Thanks," she replied, trying not to sound begrudging.

Ten minutes later, she rounded the corner of the machinery workshop to find two quads parked on the gravel in front, Levi leaning down checking the tire pressure, while Dean talked to him.

As soon as Dean caught sight of Cat, he stopped talking and gave her a hurry-up wave. Levi stood up quickly, looking slightly uncomfortable. What had he been talking about with Levi that made him look so guilty? On second thought, she didn't want to know.

Cat had grabbed her warm Stargazer coat, tied her red bandana around her neck, pulled a knit cap on her head, and found a pair of woolen mittens in the bottom of the bag she had yet to unpack. Even though they weren't going high into the mountains, there could still be patches of snow on the lower slopes.

Then she'd quickly raided the small kitchen in her and Emily's cabin, grabbing a couple of granola bars and a bottle of water. They belonged to Emily, but she hoped her friend wouldn't mind. Emily had welcomed her back with open arms, and they'd sat up and chatted long into the night. After they'd both finally gone to bed, Cat had lain awake, just enjoying the feeling of coming home. It was good to be back and even better to share a cabin with someone she could call a friend. Good friends were as scarce as hen's teeth. At least, they were in Cat's experience.

Emily could be quite particular about her stuff. At times it was almost obsessive, the way Emily kept everything in her bedroom so completely lined up and tidy. She also demanded Cat do the same in the rest of the cabin, but it was easy to overlook Emily's little flaws, because she was such a fun, vivacious person the rest of the time. Cat would stock up on a few essential items next time she was in town to pay Emily back. Cat liked to keep at least a few bars of chocolate in the cabin, and maybe some bags of candy, to feed her sweet tooth. Emily didn't care about chocolate, she preferred savory snacks, much to Cat's horror. All the staff were fed three daily meals as part of their salary, usually in the large kitchen, so they never went hungry. But Cat was a grazer, she liked to eat small meals often, so always kept a store of food available.

Hopping onto the nearest four-wheeler, she turned the key and pushed her thumb on the starter button. "I assume you know where we're headed?" she asked Levi, the first proper sentence she'd said to him all morning. It was also the first time she'd looked at him directly. Brown eyes were fastened on her, as he gazed over the top of his handlebars. Brown eyes that reminded her of dark pools of tannin-colored water, deep and enticing. Reminded her of how she'd almost drowned in them once before, got lost in their warmth, overtaken by the passion buried there. She let her gaze roam over his bronze skin and high cheekbones for a few more seconds as she waited for his answer. His Native American heritage made him all that more intriguing to her. *Had* made him intriguing, she reminded herself.

"Yes. We think the grizzly might be hiding out just over Castle Bluff, about a quarter way up Downing Mountain. In a ravine on the other side."

"Right, let's go, then," she said, pulling the knit cap down tighter over her ears and fastening the helmet over the top.

"Take him through the third gate, over in the corner of Selway's Pasture," Dean instructed, as Levi fired up his four-wheeler. "See you in a couple of hours." Her boss waved, as she led Levi up the slope and into the grassland. It was one more reason four-wheelers did so well on the ranch; they could go almost anywhere, and they were less destructive on the soil and environment than a large vehicle or truck.

The sky was overcast and grey, making the spring morning

cold and gloomy. Her woolen gloves kept the chilly air away from her fingers, but it still nipped at her nose and chin. At first, Cat's temper suited the weather. But sooner than she thought, her mood began to lift. She'd come back to Stargazer because of this amazing countryside. The lush, green grass flowed beneath their wheels as they sped over the pastures. Ahead, the Bitterroot Mountains reared up, stark and slate-colored against the sky. White caps emphasized the snow lying higher up. Levi came alongside and they rode parallel. A bubble of pleasure bloomed in her chest. Not many people got to do this as their job. Had the chance to work outdoors, ride a quad through the most beautiful country in the world. And even when she was stuck inside the machinery workshop for hours on end, it was no hardship. It was good to be back.

She couldn't help it; she smiled at Levi. And he smiled back.

They sped past a herd of cows, who bustled and mooed out of their way. They were Black Angus heifers, their hides shiny, and their brown eyes inquisitive.

A fence loomed, delineating the edge of the pasture. Tall fir trees climbed the gently rising slopes on the other side. Cat turned right and followed the fence line for a few hundred meters, until she found the third gate and hopped off her quad to open it. Struggling with the catch, she had to pull hard to work it free. Lack of use over winter had rusted it almost shut. Waving Levi through, she drove her own quad through and re-latched the gate.

Levi pulled out a folded map from a pocket inside his dark-green ranger coat. The tip of his nose was red from the cold, and she had to look away before she found herself thinking it looked cute.

"We take this one." Levi pointed to a trail heading up the incline, disappearing into the tall trees farther in. It wasn't an official trail; it'd been made by Dean and the many guests who used it over the years. During the summer, this trail would be used by those who wanted to go hiking, mountain biking, or horse riding. Cat had been amazed at just how many activities the ranch offered its guests. But it was a luxury resort and Dean and Naomi did everything in their power to make sure everyone had an amazing stay.

Then, of course, there was the activity they were most famous for. Stargazing. Montana wasn't called Big Sky Country for no reason. Dean had two high-powered telescopes set up in a small, specially built observatory. People often said they'd come to the ranch for the stars alone. City folk never understood, at least until they came to the country, just how many stars were actually in the sky. Like a carpet of fairy dust spread from horizon to horizon.

"I'll follow you," she replied.

The trail was dusty and relatively smooth here in the lower foothills. Soon, rocks and potholes began to appear. Then as they got higher, the trail got rougher, and it took all of Cat's focus to keep the quad climbing steadily. The quads wouldn't make it all the way up this trail, it eventually got too steep and narrow. They'd need mountain bikes if they wanted to get to the top of Downing Mountain. But for this job, the quads were perfect. Every now and then she would glance up at Levi, watching him maneuver his four-wheeler, standing up on the footrest so he could survey the land up ahead, or casting his gaze to each side, staying aware of everything around them.

Levi was good at his job, took it seriously. This was his first posting, and he'd told her once he had something to prove. As a Native American, Levi had more of an uphill battle than most people, and he wanted to show the University that'd offered him a scholarship, that they hadn't wasted their money. Growing up on Flathead Reservation, a little over fifty miles away, he loved this area since he was a child, and was delighted to be sent back to take on the running of Painted Rock state park. He was ambitious, but he also loved his country, wanted to nurture the environment where he could. She'd met him after he'd only been on the job for a week. Even back then, he'd been earnest and determined.

It was the same day he ran into a burning building to rescue her.

She shook her head, not wanting the memory to lodge in her brain.

Because if she started down that path, then she might remember all the little things about him, too. Like, how good it felt to kiss those full lips. When she lay beside him in bed and ran her finger lightly up and down his backbone as he slept. The way he tucked his pinkie finger into her palm when they held hands.

The way he could look into her eyes and seem to know what she felt right down in her soul.

CHAPTER FIVE

Levi topped the rise and halted his four-wheeler. This was Castle Bluff. The ravine had to be on the other side. He removed his helmet, slid off his quad and shook out his legs. The ride had taken less than fifteen minutes, but his thumb hurt from holding down the throttle for so long.

Cat pulled up on the flat ground next to him and removed her own helmet. When she switched off her quad, a sudden silence engulfed them. A ray of morning sun pierced the low clouds and filtered down between the branches of the fir trees, warming his back. As if on cue, they both turned around to drink in the view of the ranch laid out below. From up here the lodge was almost invisible, hidden by the folds of the hills and pastures surrounding it in a bright-green ocean of vegetation. Away in the distance, on the other side of Bitterroot Valley, was the Sapphire mountain range, much lower and less majestic than this one. Dry and rocky, but still heavily forested. He could look at this vista all day.

"This never gets old," Cat said quietly beside him.

He was surprised to hear her speak. It was the first civil thing she'd said to him all day, and it was almost as if she was reading his mind. She stood a few feet away, but even at this distance, a tingle of awareness shot through him. That burning chemistry was still there. He clenched a fist by his side. He was not going to let her affect him. Not this time.

"You don't get this view anywhere else," she said quietly, more as if she were speaking to herself.

"That's the truth," he admitted. Funny, back when he and Cat had been together, she'd never confessed to being particularly interested in the scenery, or the countryside. She'd been more concerned about her dirty, greasy machinery; her head had always been buried under the hood of a snowmobile, or she'd been clambering around underneath one of the huge tractors. Admittedly, a month wasn't long enough to really get to know someone, but it did make him wonder if something had changed with her in the past six months.

"I missed this while I was away." Cat took off her knit cap and shook out her spiky hair. Her blue eyes flicked quickly to his face and then back to the view. "And I missed the ranch, and all the people, too." She gave him one of her beautiful smiles, the one she kept under lock and key most of the time. It made his heart jittery to see it. Another ray of sunshine broke through the clouds and lit up her face, the row of rings in her ear sparkling. "Never thought I'd say that."

Neither did he. Had she missed him? *Not* going to ask that question. "I'm not surprised, this place tends to grow on you."

"Yeah." She gave her little trademark snort of derision. The one he'd grown used to when they were dating. "I thought I'd be happier in the bright lights of The Strip down in Vegas. But all those people began to annoy me. Their shallow lives and petty concerns. The constant noise and bright lights. Who would've thought?" She lifted her studded eyebrow in his direction.

"Maybe you have more country-girl in you than you think," he replied with a light laugh.

What was happening here? It almost felt like old times, like they were having a normal conversation. As if she'd never left. The urge to reach out and take her hand as they appreciated the view together was strong. He wanted to say he'd missed *her* while she was gone.

But of course, he wouldn't do that.

He didn't want to break this delicate truce they seemed to have formed, but he had a job to do.

"The ravine should be just over the top of this ridge. I'm going the rest of the way on foot. I don't want to startle the bear, if he does have a den down there. You should stay here and mind the quads. I won't be long." Levi turned back to the four-wheelers and rummaged around in his backpack to find a bottle of water.

"I'm coming with you."

Levi let out a gust of breath from between clenched teeth. Of course, she was. Because when had Cat ever done anything she was told? She'd always been so infuriating. Back then, it was something he admired about her. Her feistiness, that never-give-in attitude.

"It'd be safer if you stayed here." He knew it was futile, but he had to try.

"Why else did I come all the way up here, if it wasn't to protect you from the big ol' grizzly bear?" She winked and went to her quad, also pulling out a bottle of water and taking a drink. "Did you bring your gun?" she asked.

Aha, she wasn't completely heedless of danger.

"Of course." Like all park rangers in Montana, Levi completed the yearly law enforcement training that was compulsory for everyone in his line of work. Rangers had to be aware of so much more than just collecting people's park fees and talking to tourists. They also had to be fully trained to make arrests, investigate crimes, and assist police in the execution of warrants. As well as being fully qualified to carry and use a weapon. What Cat probably didn't realize was that a rifle was a better choice of protection against a grizzly. He'd tossed up between the two and finally settled on the pistol, hoping he didn't need to get that close. "But you know I won't fire it unless I have no other choice." There was no way he was going to shoot the grizzly; that wasn't what he was there for. He was there to protect it and make sure that, while the bear did no harm to humans, the reverse also remained true.

"Good to know. Lead on, then." Cat gestured to him with a flourish of her hand. He raised his eyes to the sky for a second.

"If you really intend to come, then please stay at least twenty feet behind me. And be as quiet as you can. No sudden movements or sounds. Okay?"

Her answer was a loud snort. At least her snarky side hadn't changed. The other thing that hadn't changed was how good she looked in a pair of blue jeans and boots. Even back at the machinery shed, when she'd been arguing with Dean, defying him, he couldn't help but notice those slim hips and long legs.

"You're the boss," she said, pulling the knit cap firmly down over her head, hiding her blonde hair under the black wool.

Levi put on a gun belt he'd had in his bag and tucked the weapon neatly into the holster. He also took out a spray can of bear deterrent and clipped that into a notch on his belt. This was his first line of defense, if they encountered the bear and it showed signs of aggression. He hoped he wouldn't have to use either of them. His mission today was to locate the bear and assess it, so it could be moved to a better site, or even put into a rehab facility.

Motioning for Cat to stay behind him, he began the descent into the ravine. Tall trees closed over them, casting long shadows in the mid-morning sunshine. There was a flash of blue high in the branches and Levi heard the song of the Mountain Bluebird above. He kept alert, constantly checking his surroundings, eyes also flickering over the ground, looking for bear spoor or any other signs that might tell him a grizzly had been through here. Like overturned boulders, or holes dug in the earth, and distinctive scratch marks in the bark of trees left by enormous claws. Cat did as he asked, and stayed behind him, creeping along as stealthily as he was.

Suddenly he saw it. A pile of bear scat. Bending down to take a closer look, he decided it probably was from the grizzly. The ravine wasn't too steep and was wider than Levi had thought from the map, so the descent wasn't as difficult as he'd imagined. As they traversed farther down, more and more signs of bear activity became apparent. He silently pointed out to Cat the large scar high up on the side of a tree nearby that showed where the bear had marked its territory. They were on the right trail. He waved his hand back at Cat, making sure she knew to keep quiet.

A large, rocky spur jutted into the ravine on the right, and Levi had to clamber over a pile of boulders to get past it. Once he was clear, he glanced back to make sure Cat was okay to scramble over, as well. He should have been paying more attention. Because when he turned back, he was brought up sharp by the sight in front of him. The area at the base of the rocky spur around a hundred feet in front of him had been churned up, the dusty earth pockmarked with many bear tracks and diggings. And there, tucked into a shallow indentation in the rocks—it couldn't be called a cave as such, more of an overhang—was a dark, furry shape.

Holy shit.

They'd found the bear.

It looked to be asleep.

As quietly as he could, he took a step back, and then

another, as slowly as his pounding heart would let him. Raising his hand behind him, he put it up in the air as a signal for Cat to stop.

Chancing a quick glance behind, he saw Cat had also halted in her tracks on top of the pile of boulders. As he watched, she slid behind a rock, so she was only partially visible. Good girl. The last thing he needed was for her to come barreling down the ravine, upsetting the bear.

Not taking his eyes off the animal, Levi took another step backward, at the same time pulling the bear spray off his belt.

The pile of fur quivered, and then a beady eye regarded him from deep in the shadows.

Uh-oh.

He waved urgently at Cat, hoping she would get the message, and start backtracking as fast as she could.

Suddenly, the bear was up on its feet, standing just outside the shelter of its den. The large mouth opened to reveal many white teeth, and the bear swung from side to side, scenting the air.

Levi kept stepping back, slowly and carefully, avoiding eye contact with the grizzly. The bear was checking him out, but it wasn't being overly aggressive. Yet.

Even as he backed away, Levi was assessing the bear as much as he could without looking at it directly. It was a male —Levi could tell because of the sheer size of the animal—and its head was massive, broad and square across the jaw. It was also injured. There was something wrong with the beast's face. A large, partly-healed scar ran down the left cheek and across the eye. It looked like the grizzly was blind on that side. The damage had probably been done in a fight, and probably last year, during mating season. But it was hard to tell from this distance. At least Levi now knew why the bear had taken to raiding the ranch. He'd be unable to hunt effectively, with that much damage to his sight and his jaw.

Levi's heel hit the edge of a rock, and he began to climb backward up the way he'd just come down. This was going to be nearly impossible to climb the rocks without turning around. He didn't want to turn his back on the animal.

"I'll watch it, you climb." Cat's voice was low and urgent. But even that quiet whisper was enough to elicit a low, huffing sound from the bear, which meant it was warning them to stay away.

He didn't have much choice. If he were to climb over the pile of boulders, he'd need to trust Cat to watch his back for him, warn him if the bear charged. Should he unholster his gun? Levi took another quick look at the bear. Grizzlies were notoriously unpredictable, but this one hadn't advanced on them since he'd stood up. Levi guessed the poor thing was in a lot of pain and wouldn't attack them unless provoked.

He turned his back and began to climb, keeping the bear spray in his left hand. The back of his neck prickled and sweat ran freely down his spine. If the bear charged now, he probably wouldn't stand a chance. Cat muttered half-heard encouragement as he climbed, and it was the sound of her voice, more than anything, that kept him going.

When he got to the top of the rock scramble, he motioned Cat to precede him down the other side, and then they made their way as quickly and quietly as possible back up the ravine, glancing behind every now and then to make sure they weren't being followed.

When he thought it was safe, Levi finally let them stop, and both of them leaned over with their hands on their knees, sucking in air after their fast climb.

"Fuck, Levi, that was close." A large grin split Cat's face, even as she said the words. Levi was thunderstruck. She seemed to have got a kick out of the whole encounter.

"Yes, it was. Grizzlies are bloody dangerous. So, you need to stop looking like you've just been on the best carnival ride at the fair," he said through indrawn breaths. "That was serious back there, Cat."

"You have to admit, it was a bit of a rush, though," she replied. "Besides, I trust you to keep me safe."

Was she ever going to change? Was she always going to treat life with reckless abandon, as if she were invincible? Or was it just that he was too serious? His blood was pumping madly through his veins, the adrenaline only now beginning to fade. He dissected the past few minutes in his head. He hadn't been afraid. If anything, he'd been more worried about Cat getting hurt. More worried about having to shoot the bear, if it came to that. Which would've been sad. But now they were safe, and on their way back up the mountain. It felt good to be alive. Maybe she was right, or perhaps a little of her devil-may-care attitude had rubbed off on him. He'd never admit it, but the past few minutes had been *a bit of a rush*, as she put it. Not that he would ever put himself—or Cat—in danger on purpose.

"Come on, let's get out of here." He couldn't help it, he flashed her a smile, and her face lit up in a cheeky grin in return.

CHAPTER SIX

Cat followed Levi's dust trail all the way down the bluff. They'd decided to stop when they reached the bottom and have some lunch. Far away from the annoyed bear in the ravine. She was still buzzing from their close encounter. Poor thing, it'd been badly injured; no wonder it was turning to the easy food source down on the ranch.

Cat enjoyed the feel of the cool air whipping against her cheeks as they descended through the trees. She'd never admit this to Dean but being out riding had been better than being stuck in the machinery workshop all morning.

Sooner than she thought, they were down onto the grassland, the fence lining the border of Stargazer Ranch looming in front of them. Levi pulled up next to a patch of grass. She turned off her quad and watched him surreptitiously as he stomped around, flattening a spot on the grass to sit, and then unpacking his bag.

Her body was already re-acquainting itself with his, and it seemed there was nothing she could do about it. She found her gaze lingering on his broad back and shoulders as she followed him down the ravine this morning. Tracing the outline of strong legs and that cute butt as he rock-hopped downwards. It was almost as if her fingers remembered the feel of his skin. And her arms remembered holding Levi close, his body against hers. That oh-so-familiar smell, that was purely Levi.

She grabbed her own bag and sat down at least two feet away from him. She didn't care if she seemed rude. Call it self-preservation, whatever you liked, but she needed to keep some distance between them. Sifting through the contents of her bag, she dropped a granola bar and a bottle of water on the grass in front of her.

"You can share my lunch, if you like. I made two sandwiches this morning."

Cat looked down at her lonely bar and then across at Levi's food. Were they cheese and pickle, one of her favorites? She opened her mouth to say no, when her stomach rumbled loudly.

He grinned and handed one over without a word. Had he known she was going to be here and made the sandwiches especially? Was he in on this plan as much as Dean? Cat eyed him warily as he took a large bite, ignoring her pointed glare. Levi had looked as shocked as she had when Dean told them Cat was going with him. So, either he was a really good actor, or…

Nope, he hadn't planned this, she finally decided. Cat bit into the sandwich, the fresh white bread melting in her mouth along with the salty tang of the cheese. It was a proven fact; there was nothing better than eating a cheese and pickle sandwich while sitting in the sun, enjoying the peaceful wilderness. Why had she never truly appreciated this before?

"Good, huh?" he asked through a mouthful.

"Yes, thank you." Then, as an afterthought, she added, "I've got two granola bars. We can have one each for dessert."

"Great." His face lit up with a smile, and Cat's heart hiccupped in her chest.

Shit.

After six months apart, she'd managed to convince herself that the fling with Levi was dead and buried. He was completely out of her system. But after only a few hours in his company, she knew that was complete bullshit.

How was she going to do this? Keep working at Stargazer while pretending Levi didn't affect her; that he didn't matter to her anymore.

"What are you going to do with the grizzly?" she asked.

"I'll organize a specialist wildlife team to come take a look. He'll have to be rehabilitated, first. We can't relocate him or put him back in the wild until those injuries are healed. He'd just start raiding farms or towns again. There's a wildlife center run by my department, over in Helena, that takes in rescued bears."

"Poor thing. I never thought I'd say this, but I actually felt sorry for him. He looked like one of those gladiators from back in the Roman days. All beaten and bloody, but ready to fight to the death. I hope you can help him."

"They're beautiful creatures. And they have as much right to exist as we do," Levi replied, a slightly bemused look on his face, as if she'd said something to surprise him.

They talked for many more minutes about how the bear would need to be tranquilized and then moved. It'd be a complicated job. Levi's devotion to his job and his country had always impressed Cat. One of the many things she'd liked about him was that he genuinely cared. About the environment and about people. Especially about his own people, the Salish Tribe, over on Flathead Reservation. Even Levi admitted his people's problems were many and complicated, but he hoped to help them towards a better future.

Perhaps she was finally starting to glean what he saw in all this, why he loved this area so much.

"Speaking of critters," Levi said. "You'd like my new pal. His name's Rekker." Cat laughed at the crazy name. But when Levi started to describe the escapades of his tame raccoon, Cat soon understood. Levi had nursed him back to health after he'd been attacked, possibly by a mountain lion. Most people around this area saw raccoons as a pest, because they were known to carry rabies, amongst other things. So, Levi didn't normally divulge the fact he had one living in his backyard. Cat was glad he trusted her enough to let her in on it.

"I love the name." She reached over and grabbed the crumpled paper from both their sandwiches and dropped it into her backpack. "So, you keep him locked up in a cage at night?"

"Yeah, because he's so tame, and he still walks with a limp, it's not safe for him to stay out at night. He's too trusting, and not worldly-wise enough to survive out there on his own. Most of the other raccoons in the area have rejected him, because he's got the stink of human all over him."

"Oh, that's a little bit sad."

"I know, but it's also life. If I didn't help him, he would've died. I'm hoping to release him back into the wild one day; raccoons don't make the best pets and he is a native animal, after all," Levi said, absently handing her the granola bar wrapper, as well. Her heart stopped beating. It was such a simple gesture. So perfectly normal. So much like they were a normal couple, who did this kind of thing every day. "He's so funny, sometimes he—" Levi stopped, mid-sentence and stared at something over Cat's left shoulder. "Is that smoke?"

Cat whipped her head around. Then stood so she could see better.

A large funnel of dark-grey smoke was indeed heading skyward.

"Where's it coming from?" Levi barked.

The grasslands were laid out before them, green and hilly. Behind that was a dip in the ground, with a large stand of trees blocking their view. The lodge lay much farther over to the right, in the middle of the pastures.

"I'm not sure," she admitted. "But we have a couple of cabins in that valley." Holy shit, surely not. Surely there couldn't be another fire on Stargazer Ranch. Not on the first day she returned to work.

Cat ran over and unlocked the gate, then jumped on her quad and gunned it though the opening, not even bothering with her helmet.

"Wait. Cat, wait," Levi shouted after her. But she had to get there. Had to know if this was one of their cabins on fire. She left Levi to shut the gate behind them, as she raced over the pastures toward the smoke. The trees loomed larger, still blocking her view of what was going on beyond them. She rode fast, leaning down over the handlebars and urging the four-wheeler on, not caring that the quad became airborne more than once as she flew over a hump. Every now and then, she caught a glimpse of the bright-orange flicker of flames. How far behind was Levi? She had no idea and didn't want to chance a glance behind her.

Bouncing over a lump in the grass, Cat hardly slowed the machine as she turned onto one of the resort's internal roads. It was a loop road that serviced three of their luxury cabins. She roared past the driveway to the first cabin, which was tucked into the edge of the tree line that'd been blocking her view. Cat caught sight of a couple standing on their porch, gawping at the growing tower of smoke.

The second cabin was around the side of a small hill. All the cabins were isolated and private, designed so the occupants couldn't see any of their neighbors. When she rounded the bend in the road, the sight she'd been dreading invaded her senses.

The beautiful cabin was fully alight. It brought the memories from seven months ago flooding back, when she'd run into another of the Stargazer cabins to save a dog. This couldn't be happening. Not again. It was too surreal.

She skidded to a halt on the gravel driveway, right in front of the main steps leading up to the wrap-around porch. The whole front of the building was ablaze, as if the fire had started at the front door.

"I've called the fire department," Levi shouted, as he pulled up beside her four-wheeler. She heard him but didn't acknowledge his words.

Cat jogged around the side of the cabin. Was anyone still in there? She racked her brain to try and remember if cabin nineteen had been occupied last night. But it was no good, she hadn't been back on the ranch long enough to know where all the guests were staying.

Cat tried to peer in one of the side windows. The glass was blackened with soot and smoke. It was impossible to tell if anyone was in there. She jogged farther around, to the back of the cabin. The flames hadn't reached this far yet, but the smoke was billowing all around. The back door was locked when she tried it. Lifting a booted foot, she slammed it against the lock. There was a crack, but the door didn't budge. She kicked it again, with all her might, the shock of her foot connecting with the solid, wooden door traveling all the way up her leg. But there was another satisfying crack, and this time, the door flew open. She pulled her bandana up over her mouth and nose and checked that her knit cap was sitting firmly on her head. At least she was better protected this time as she raced into the burning building.

"Cat, don't you dare go in there." Levi appeared around the side of the cabin, but his warning was almost lost over the roar of the flames.

"There might be someone inside," she yelled over her

shoulder.

"Don't you dare…" The rest of his words receded as she dove into the building.

It was dark. And smoky. And searing hot.

"Is anyone in here?" she shouted. "Answer me, if you can hear me." There was nothing apart from the crackle and hiss of burning wood.

Cat ran into the kitchen, which was always situated at the back of each cabin. All the cabins on the property were built to the exact same design. Her vision was limited because of the smoke. But after a few seconds, she determined it was empty.

The second bedroom was across the hall and she ducked into it, calling out as she went. It took longer to search this room, as she hunched down to make sure no one was under the bed and opened the door to check in the large closet.

"Cat, what the fuck?" Levi's voice came from the doorway. She could only make out his smudged outline against the light coming through the back door.

"I just need to check the other bedroom," she said, pushing past him.

"This is crazy," he yelled. Yet, he followed her down the hall. They were both coughing loudly, and Cat could hardly see, the smoke stung her eyes so much. But before she made it even half-way down the hall, flames bellowed and belched out of both rooms at the front of the cabin. The heat intensified, and even when Cat put a hand up to shield her face, it was nearly more than she could bear.

There was a loud pop and then an explosion, glass and wood flying everywhere. Cat was blown backwards, landing on Levi as they both crashed to the floor. More flaming wood collapsed around them. She felt Levi scramble to his feet behind her, then he gripped her under the arms, dragging her with him as he backed down what remained of the hallway.

They emerged outside into the relatively clean air, coughing and spluttering.

He dragged her fifty feet away from the burning building, before he turned her around to face him. "Are you okay? Are you burned? Tell me you're okay." His face was twisted into a grimace of despair, his eyes darting all over her body, checking her for injury.

"I'm okay. I'm okay," she repeated, also scanning him for any cuts or burns. Apart from a whole lot of black soot smudged on his face, he looked fine.

Levi hauled her in and crushed her against his chest.

And she let him, resting her nose in the crook of his neck. Breathing in his protection and strength. Something inside loosened at his touch. Something she'd been holding on to so tight for the past six months. Like her mind was finally giving her body permission to give in. It was nice not to have to be solely responsible for her own welfare. To have someone willing to take care of her.

They stood like that for many seconds, until the arm Cat had used to shield herself from the flames began to sting like hell. Maybe she wasn't completely unscathed, after all. And what if there had been guests inside the cabin? Perhaps overcome by the smoke and lying in the front bedroom. Just like Levi had been the day she rescued him from his burning house. She shuddered at the thought she may have failed. She'd never forgive herself if a life had been lost today.

Levi tensed, then pushed her away, holding her at arm's length so he could stare her in the face. "Holy mother of… I swear Cat, if you do that one more time… I'll…"

"You'll what, Levi?" The feeling of intimacy over their shared embrace evaporated in a puff of anger. "I didn't need rescuing, you know."

"Oh, for fuck's sake, are we really doing this again?" he accused loudly.

CHAPTER SEVEN

Dean's distraught voice cut through the retort Levi knew Cat had been about to spit out. But he almost didn't care anymore. Couldn't she see what she'd done? How her actions affected everyone, not just her?

"Cat, Levi, where are you?" Dean rounded the corner of the burning cabin like a mini hurricane, a look of pure terror on his face. "Oh, thank God." He ran up to them. "I saw your quads out the front, and then something exploded in the cabin as I got out of the truck, and I thought…"

They both knew what he thought.

Levi stepped away from Cat. "We were inside but got out. We're both okay."

"I was checking to make sure no one was in the building." Cat cast Levi an anguished glance. "But the flames drove me…us…back before we could check the front rooms. Someone could still be—"

"The Fergusons are all out on the cattle drive with Emily. If you'd waited a few more seconds, I could've told you that."

Both he and Cat let out simultaneous sighs of relief. No one had died in the inferno.

Cat spoke into the sudden silence. "If I'd waited, and someone was in there… What then, Dean?"

"I see your point," he agreed with a begrudging nod of his head. "Look, I commend your bravery." Dean let out a gust of agitated breath. "Both of you." He glanced at Levi. "But…"

"But what?" Cat cut in.

"I don't want to lose one of my employees, either." Dean's normally jovial face was set into hard lines. "I care about you. I have a duty to keep you safe. The smart thing would've been to wait for the firefighters, Cat." At least Dean was on the same page as Levi. But he worried even Dean's words wouldn't sink through Cat's thick skull.

Right on cue, she gave her trademark snort of derision. But it was half-hearted, as if Cat didn't really mean it.

Dean shook his head and turned his gaze to the flaming building. "I can't believe this is happening again." The heat was so intense, Levi took a few steps backward and the others followed suit. Levi had been so caught up in the drama unfolding before him, he only now had time to think about the repercussions of the fire. There'd been no arson attempts in the past six months. What were the odds that the day after Cat returned to work at the ranch, another cabin burned to the ground? It seemed like more than just coincidence. But Cat had been with him the whole morning, so he could vouch for her whereabouts. Which left only one alternative. Clayton must be back. But why would Cat be his intended target? Dean, and his ranch, were the targets of the arsonist. At least, that's what everyone thought.

He glanced over at her. Was she nursing her arm?

"You did hurt yourself," he accused loudly. "Let me see."

She backed away, but not quickly enough to escape his grasp, and he caught her by the wrist.

"It's nothing." She tried to pull free, pursing her lips in denial.

She still had on her Stargazer coat, but the weatherproof material was singed and blackened from her wrist to her elbow. "One of the burning bits of wood must've fallen on me. But it's okay, the coat saved me."

"I'll be the judge of that," Levi growled, then gently pulled the coat sleeve up her arm. She was wearing a plaid shirt underneath, but, surprisingly, it was only lightly singed. He had to undo the buttons at the wrist so he could roll the shirt up, until her arm was finally exposed.

It was hard to see the exact damage because of Cat's tattoos, but dark bruises were already forming. One particular spot was red and angry, which must've been where the burning wood had scorched all the way through. He examined her arm, taking care not to touch the burned section. It didn't look too bad. Cat was right, the coat had pretty much saved her.

Her arm was warm against his palm, her wrist bones surprisingly slim and bird-like as he circled it easily with his thumb and forefinger.

"Should I call an ambulance?" Dean asked. He'd been watching with a worried frown, as Levi examined her.

"No," Cat declared. But Dean didn't even glance her way, instead waiting for Levi's proclamation.

After one final inspection, Levi said, "No, she'll be fine. We need some water to cool it down, though."

"I've got a bottle in my truck." Dean jogged away to the front of the house and Cat rolled her eyes at Levi. Which again had Levi wondering. Normally, she would've jumped down Dean's throat for not listening to her; told him she was more than capable of making her own decisions.

More cars could be heard pulling up in the road below the cabin, loud, panicked voices shouting over the roar of the flames.

"Come on. Let's stop anyone else, before they try and rush in to check the building," Levi said, following in Dean's footsteps, taking a wide berth around the side of the cabin.

Another loud crash within sent more sparks and flames spiraling into the sky.

For once, Cat didn't argue. Which meant her arm was hurting her more than she'd admit. Dean met them half-way and handed Levi a large water bottle, then disappeared around the front of the cabin again. Levi drizzled the cooling water over Cat's burned arm and saw a flicker of relief cross her face.

"That's better," she admitted. Cat was almost black from head to toe. Covered in soot and ash and blackened by flames. Her blue eyes stark against her darkened face. At least she still had on her knit cap, which had saved her hair from singeing.

There were people everywhere now, some with fire extinguishers, others filling buckets of water from a hose. Levi knew the cabin was too far gone now, for any of that to work.

When the bottle of water was empty he called out to Dean, "I'm going to take Cat back to her cabin and get more water on this burn.

"Good idea," Dean called back. "Then I'll need you to come down to the lodge to talk to the police. I'm not going to sit back and let this happen to me, or the ranch, again."

Cat hopped on her quad, after first answering the concerned questions from other staff, who were arriving in a convoy of cars coming up the road, confirming she and Levi were indeed okay. By silent agreement, he followed Cat on his four-wheeler back to her small cabin, nestled near the main lodge.

She led him in the front door, again without a word, and then stopped in the middle of the small living room, as if suddenly unsure what to do next.

"Let me help you get your coat off," he said gently. She glanced up at him, a slightly dazed expression in her eyes.

Then let him undo the zipper and ease it over her shoulders. It troubled him, to see that flash of vulnerability. Cat never questioned anything she did, always seemed so totally sure of herself. Her reckless streak was constantly driving her to do incredibly stupid, incredibly brave things. Today, however, it seemed the fire had freaked her out.

Levi eased his own ranger coat off and dropped both garments on the nearest chair. His boss wouldn't be pleased to hear Levi had ruined yet *another* jacket.

"Where's all your first-aid stuff?"

"In the bathroom," she replied, taking a few hesitant steps in that direction.

"Let's go and have a look at your arm." He brushed past her and walked into the bathroom, opening the cupboards above the sink, looking for bandages and ointment. For two girls sharing a cabin, the place was decidedly uncluttered. Actually, it was so tidy it was almost disturbing. Levi knew it wasn't Cat who kept the place clean, he'd experienced her messy side firsthand during their short fling. It must be Emily who kept the place so orderly.

Levi turned on the faucet and gently placed Cat's arm under the cooling flow of water. She sat down on the edge of the tub, watching him, eyes wide and still a little vacant. There was a small first aid kit tucked into the back below the sink, and he pulled it out, searching for what he needed.

Levi knelt on the floor in front of her and without even asking, he began to unbutton her plaid shirt. "We need to get this off." She did nothing to stop him. His fingers remembered doing this very same thing so many times before. The first time they'd made love, he'd helped her take off her shirt, and she'd returned the favor. Back then, it'd been a hurried affair, their passion for each other almost overwhelming.

She winced as he carefully drew the fabric over her burned

arm. Then he gently tugged her white T-shirt over her head. Cat always wore a tank top underneath, another layer of warmth against the cool spring weather. Cat never wore a bra —she always said bras were horribly uncomfortable, and her small, pert breasts didn't need the support. He thought her breasts beautiful and told her every occasion he'd had. Sitting on the edge of her tub with only a tank top on, her arm still under the running water, her bare shoulders pale in the harsh fluorescent light of the bathroom, blonde hair streaked with black, she looked suddenly lost and unguarded. The tattoos normally gave her a rock-chick kind of vibe. And he'd loved that about her. But today, they made her look more vulnerable. The urge to take her in his arms struck him. Without giving himself time to second-guess the feeling, he reached up and enfolded her in his embrace. For the second time today, she didn't resist. In fact, her arms came up and wrapped around his back, pulling him in closer. They stayed like that, him kneeling on the hard, tiled floor, her sitting on the tub, for uncounted moments.

The words, *I missed you*, hovered on his lips.

Cat spoke unexpectedly, her words muffled because she was speaking into his chest. "Today, when I was in that cabin, I kept remembering the time you were unconscious, lying in your house." An almost undetectable shudder ran through her.

It was the closest Cat was going to come to admitting she'd been scared. Which was interesting. He wasn't sure how to answer her.

He drew back a little, so he could look into her eyes, try and figure out what was going on in her head. Cat licked her lips and Levi's eyes were instantly drawn to her mouth. That saucy, sassy mouth of hers. He suddenly became acutely aware of Cat, of how she felt in his arms, her mere presence setting off all his body's long-suppressed yearnings.

Silence hovered between them.

Her gaze flickered down to his mouth and then back up to pierce him with their crystalline blue.

It was too much for him to resist.

He leaned in, letting his lips press against hers. She met him halfway, her mouth soft at first, but soon deepening the kiss, luring him in. He wanted to melt into her. Hunger flared, exactly as it had before. Time hadn't dulled his need for her. If anything, it'd sharpened it. She ignited something deep within him no other woman had been able to. A need that was almost a physical pain.

His hands were already lifting the edge of her tank top, drawing it over her head, being careful not to knock her sore arm. As if unable to wait for him to finish, she grabbed the clothing and tugged the last bit over her head.

His gaze roamed over her heavenly body. Trim, slim-hipped, almost elfin, with her small breasts and narrow waist. Cat let him gaze his fill, encouraging him with her eyes. She was the one who brought his hand up to cover one of her breasts, gasping as his fingers closed around it.

It was easy to ignore that tiny voice of caution in his head, warning him he'd sworn he wasn't going here again with Cat. After all, he was an adult. He could do this. Control his emotions enough so as not to let Cat under his skin this time. It was also easy to ignore the voice when it asked why Cat was doing this. Had she missed him as much as he'd missed her? Had she been fighting her feelings, as well? And at this moment in time, did it really matter? He wanted her so bad, his cock bulged against the fabric of his pants.

Chemistry had never been a problem between them. The sex was great, out of this world, even. They lit each other up like a sky full of fireworks. Their problem had been Cat's inability to commit. But right now, Levi wasn't worried about Cat's staying power, because his body was humming with untamed need.

He stood, dragging Cat up with him. Fumbling with his own shirt, he tried to undo the buttons one-handed, while making sure his mouth stayed firmly on Cat's. At the same time, she used her good hand to attempt to undo his belt, and then he felt the zipper of his pants being drawn down. He was rock hard. She ran her hand down the length of him and her touch was so familiar, he shivered. A small murmur of appreciation came from Cat and he thought he would explode with need.

Finally, his shirt lay in a heap on the floor, his pants along with them, as he reveled in the feel of her skin, smooth and supple on his. He wasn't sure how it happened, but Cat's jeans were suddenly somehow down around her ankles, and he had pushed her up against the bathroom wall. She was stroking him, pulling him toward her, then guiding him in. The feeling as he entered her was pure, unadulterated ecstasy. Nothing else existed in this world, except him and Cat. She cried out his name as he entered, and he was almost driven crazy by the sound. She'd never held back in the bedroom. But it'd also never been this hot and needy, this quick and dirty, before.

It was over almost as quickly as it started. Cat convulsed in his arms, digging her nails into his back. And he followed her, release like a tumbling avalanche. Perhaps he should've asked her if she was still on the pill. But she would've stopped him if she weren't.

They stayed locked together, Cat's head thrown back against the wall as he panted heavily, trying to catch his breath.

CHAPTER EIGHT

What had she done? She closed her eyes and let the water run over her shoulders and down her back, keeping her injured arm away from the warm droplets. Thankfully, the burn wasn't bad, Levi had pronounced it as most likely only a first-degree burn, no worse than a bad sunburn.

Levi was waiting in the living room for her. She needed to pull herself together and get out of the shower. Turning the taps, she grabbed a towel from the hanger and stepped onto the mat. At least she looked better now, she thought, examining herself in the mirror. The sooty trails of ash were no longer running down her cheeks, and her hair had returned to its normal, golden color.

Looking down at her pile of clothes on the floor, she grimaced. She'd forgotten to get clean clothes before taking a shower. And these were too dirty to wear again; they smelled like she'd smoked a thousand cigarettes.

Closing her eyes, she gritted her teeth, then wrapped the towel around herself. She could either ask Levi to get her some clothes, or walk right past him, wearing only her towel. But after what they'd done together in the bathroom, it wasn't that Levi would see her half-naked that was worrying her. More like, because of what they'd just done, she felt like he would see straight though her. She'd been stupid, and let him back in. Give a man an inch, and he'd take a mile. Even though a part of her knew Levi wasn't like that. She was tarring him with the same brush as the hundreds of other men she'd met, and he was different. Which was one of the reasons she needed to stay away from him.

Straightening her shoulders, she yanked the door open and stepped out as if she owned the place—which she technically did—and as if Levi hadn't turned around to watch her with his deep-brown eyes as she made her way into her bedroom. She didn't slam the door, rather liked to think she closed it quickly behind her with a sigh of relief.

"Hurry up," Levi called through the door. "We still have to fix up your arm, and then get down to the lodge."

It was harder than she thought to dress one-handed. And getting the shirt sleeve over her burned and bruised arm was excruciating. Maybe it'd be better once it was bandaged. At least it wouldn't rub against the fabric.

Time to put her Cat persona back in place. She drew in a deep breath and held it for a couple of seconds. She could do this. Pretend that nothing major had happened between them. That Levi didn't affect her one little bit. All business, she opened her bedroom door and gave Levi a smile. He returned a tentative smile, then led her toward the bathroom. She hesitated and then followed. *Pretend you didn't just have hot, dirty sex in that very same bathroom.*

He was quiet as he sorted through the first aid kit, pulling out a tube of aloe and some bandages, while she once more sat on the edge of the tub.

She wanted to say something to break the tense atmosphere. But the only thoughts rolling around in her head included him kissing her fiercely on the mouth, or her with her back against the wall and her jeans around her ankles. She almost groaned out loud in mortification. Levi's beard had been a revelation. It looked good on him, but she hadn't been sure if it would be kissable. The sensation hadn't been unpleasant; it was a lot softer than she imagined. And to be truthful, she'd been so caught up in the passion connecting them, she hadn't really cared.

The silence between them deepened. He motioned for her to hold out her arm.

"Cat, can I ask you a question?" He didn't look up, still intent on his ministrations.

"It depends," she answered, wary of where he might be going with this.

"Does Clayton have something against you? Do you think he lit the fire as a warning to you?" As Levi spoke, he applied the ointment, and she sucked in a painful breath. It gave her the time she needed to gather her thoughts. The same thought had occurred to her. This couldn't be a coincidence. Because it was her first day back at work. And it was the first fire in six months.

"I've been trying to come up with an answer to the same question," she replied, shaking her head. "But I can't think of anything. I didn't have a lot to do with Clayton, back when I worked at Stargazers last time. He worked the horses and the cattle, and I stayed in the machinery workshop. Our paths barely crossed, unless it was at mealtimes." It was true, Clayton had hardly even registered on her radar most of the time. "He was a bit loud and arrogant. Came across as brash, and sometimes even downright rude. But he was never violent, that I remember."

"You two never argued, had any kind of disagreement?" Levi still wasn't looking at her, kept his focus on the pristine, white bandage he was wrapping around her arm. The ointment must have a cooling agent in it, because her forearm was already feeling better. If only Levi's gentle touch on her skin didn't make her want to jump every time his fingers grazed her wrist.

"Nope." She couldn't think of anything else to tell him.

Finally, he looked up and met her gaze. "I believe you, of course I do. But I need to warn you, if I'm thinking along these lines, you can bet the cops will be, too."

"I thought Clayton was the only suspect," she said, a little too loudly. "Do you think I'm a suspect now?" She sat up straighter, suddenly alarmed.

"No, no, of course not. Besides, I'm your alibi for today, even if they do."

She studied his face for many long seconds but saw only sincerity. Her heart was beating fast now. She hadn't even considered she might be under suspicion. His brown eyes showed only quiet candor, and some of her fear subsided.

"I'm warning you, however, that the police will want to follow every angle on this. They'll want to delve into your history." He sighed and stood. "What I'm trying to say, Cat, is you need to tread lightly. You know, keep that feisty tongue of yours in check."

She narrowed her eyes at him. "I'll say whatever I damn well please." She'd had dealings with the police before, and she wasn't a fan of the cops. Because of the way she looked, the way she dressed, and the way she rode her motorcycle, she attracted more than her fair share of attention from the law. And they hadn't endeared themselves to her in any way. Most of them were far too quick to judge her on her appearance. She'd always stayed on the right side of the law, never stolen anything, or hurt anyone. But that often didn't seem to matter to a young cop on a power trip, or an old cop whose prejudiced eyes couldn't see past the fact she was a woman who liked to ride a motorcycle.

"Cat, please listen to me. The last thing you want to do is antagonize the cops."

"I know how to handle myself, but thanks for the input."

Cat got up and stalked out of the bathroom.

"I'm only trying to help." Levi came after her.

Goddammit, now she felt like a major bitch. How was it Levi always managed to push her buttons? He always seemed to have the moral high ground. He was right, not that she was going to admit it. She did have a fiery temper. And perhaps she needed to learn to contain it better. He *was* trying to help her. It was partly those high morals of his that attracted her in the first place. He was inherently a good man, trying to do good things in this world. Even after the way he grew up, and even now, the way he was sometimes treated by ignorant people, he managed to rise above it all. She respected him for that. Even while it irritated her, because she could never be like that. One more reason she needed to stay away from Levi. She would only bring him down to her level.

"Let's go." Leaving the singed Stargazer coat where Levi had thrown it, she took her own waterproof coat down from its hanger on the back of the door. Levi's coat was also blackened and singed in places. All because he'd followed her into a burning building.

It took them less than a minute on the four-wheelers to make it down the slope from her cabin and park at the back of the lodge. Through the trees, she could see two cruisers parked in the main parking lot. Two cars. It meant the cops were taking this seriously.

Levi strode past her, pushing the door to the kitchen open and then holding it for her. A blast of cold air followed her in. "Let's get this over with," he growled.

Big Tom was sitting in the kitchen, nursing a cup of coffee. "They're in the main conference room." He pointed toward the front of the lodge. "They're waiting for you," he warned. But before either Levi or Cat took two steps toward the door, Tom stood up and blocked their path. "You both okay? I heard what you did. Rushed into a burning building. Again."

Tom's strong jaw was clenched, his deep brow furrowed.

"Thanks, Tom," Cat said, laying a hand on his broad shoulder. His worried gaze spoke volumes. They were all anxious that the arsonist was back. "We're both fine."

Levi nodded his head in agreement.

"Naomi said we'll get the staff together at dinner and have a debrief. We need to figure out what's going on." Big Tom sat back down, leaving the way clear for them to proceed.

"That's a good idea," Cat agreed. "See you then." She didn't look back, but she knew Tom's troubled gaze followed them, as they walked down the hall.

For the next two hours, Cat spent most of the time holding down her growing temper. They were introduced to the two law enforcement officers, Deputy Jude Wilder and Deputy Susan Nomad. Sheriff Hank Buchanan was busy with a case of car theft back in town, so, Deputy Jude took charge. Firstly, he double-checked that both she and Levi were unharmed after the fire. Cat's arm throbbed a little, but the aloe seemed to be doing the job. She shrugged and said they were both fine. Jude narrowed his eyes at her, but after a few seconds he went on with his debrief. He revealed there were a few lines of questioning they were following, and not all of them included Clayton, which irritated Cat. Surely Clayton should be their only suspect? Levi had identified him as the person who bashed him unconscious on the night his house was set on fire.

When she brought this up, Deputy Wilder looked at her sideways and told her Levi had confirmed that it *looked* like Clayton. The person had been wearing his hat and coat. But Levi admitted it'd been dark, and he couldn't confirm one-hundred-percent it was Clayton. All they had was circumstantial evidence, at best.

Levi had said nothing to dispute this, just raised his eyebrows at her. Cat couldn't believe the police thought it might be anyone else. Of course, it was Clayton. He hadn't been seen since the fire at Levi's house, and his truck had been found wrecked on a country road not far from there on the same day. Circumstantial evidence her ass, she snorted in disgust.

Naomi was asked to come up with a list of any guests who might've been staying at the ranch now, as well as six months ago, when the previous fires occurred. She'd been surprised to learn from the records there was one such guest, a gentleman by the name of Mike Spencer, vacationing alone in cabin thirteen. He supposedly loved to come up here for the solitude, leaving his family at home. It gave him breathing space from his high-stress job as a CEO of some Wall Street Company. Deputy Wilder took his name and contact details, and said they'd talk to him next.

Deputy Wilder drilled both Dean and Naomi about any emails or strange texts they might've received recently. They all knew about the anonymous, threatening email Dean received last year. But Jude wanted him to go through it again, as well as list anyone else who might hold a grudge against him. The list wasn't long; it only contained three people.

Mathew Davis, the man they'd bought the ranch from fifteen years ago. He'd been on the brink of bankruptcy and was being forced to sell before the bank foreclosed on him, but the sale almost hadn't gone through because Mathew had tried to disrupt it at every turn. In the end, the man had become bitter and abusive, almost as if he blamed Dean for his bad fortune.

"We haven't seen Mathew in years, though," Naomi mused. "He used to turn up, unannounced and walk around like he still owned the place. Kept saying he should never have sold the ranch, and one day he was going to get it back."

"I felt sorry for him," Dean added quietly. "He really loved this property. He poured his heart and soul into it, but it wasn't enough."

"Yes, he did." Naomi laid a hand on Dean's shoulder. "But he wasn't a nice man, not really. I always found him arrogant and obsequious. His business acumen had a lot to be desired. And his jealousy over how we managed to turn Stargazer into a profitable ranch isn't our problem, either."

"You're right," Dean sighed. "I guess it definitely puts him on our suspicious persons list."

The second suspect was an old girlfriend of Dean's, Summer Donovan. She'd stalked him for many years after they broke up, constantly asking him for money, especially after he became a billionaire, making it rich with his technology company in Silicon Valley.

"Poor Summer," Dean said. "She was under some delusion that we never really split up. Kept saying we'd made something special together. And when I discovered the truth, I'd come running back. Said she had something of mine, and she wasn't going to return it, unless I came to see her in person." He turned to gaze out the window, his eyes glazing over, as old memories took hold.

Naomi picked up the conversation. "I'm not sure *poor Summer* is the description I'd use," she said sourly. "Even years later, well after I met Dean, she was still sending him texts, sometimes three or four a day. I eventually talked him into getting a restraining order to stop her."

"We'll get our people in LA onto her immediately," Jude said. "If we get any details, we'll update you." He glanced down at the list Dean had given him. The last guy is called Donald Garcia, is that right?"

"Yes," Dean replied. "I employed him to do the marketing at my Silicon Valley tech company, way back before we bought the ranch. I had to fire him in the end, as his work was shoddy and second-rate. But then the guy threatened to take me to court for unfair dismissal. Can you believe it?" Dean raised his eyebrows, as if it still surprised him. "And then he proceeded to try and sell some of my trade secrets to my competitors. Donald was black banned from the industry after that, unable to get a job anywhere in The Valley. Last I heard, he moved to Michigan," Dean said. "Got a job with Ford Motor Company, working as some lowly warehouse manager. He's married, with three kids. I can't see him being involved, not now he's got a family to look after. Can you?" Dean addressed his question to the deputy.

Deputy Wilder raised a skeptical eyebrow. "On the contrary, if this guy has hit rock-bottom, he could still be blaming you for his fall from grace. The one thing I've learned in this job, is to never underestimate anyone. You'd be surprised what people are capable of."

Dean sat quietly after that, perhaps digesting the deputy's declaration. Poor Dean. He always wanted to see the good in people. Cat was a little surprised there were so many slightly unbalanced people out there, all with some grudge against Dean. But then, the world was a crazy place. Was it likely any of these three were involved? Cat just wasn't sure.

"Could there be any connection to your other ranch? The one in Australia?" Deputy Wilder asked.

Dean shook his head. "I don't believe so, but I've contacted Daniella—that's my sister—to let her know what's going on and to make sure she keeps alert to anything out of the ordinary over there."

The deputy was happy with that, but still asked for Daniella's contact details, so they could ask her a few questions.

Then he began to question Cat. About where she'd been for the past six months and details of her employer in Vegas.

"What about your family? Where are they? We might want to talk to them, if you don't mind." Wilder kept his gaze mild but couldn't quite hide the glint of sharp interest in his eyes.

"I do mind," she growled. "I don't know where my father is. And I don't really care." Levi was the only one who knew anything about her relationship with her father. It really irked her Wilder was making her air her dirty laundry in front of everyone. "Before you ask, no, I don't have a mother. She died when I was really young. I've got no brothers or sisters, either."

Naomi made a small sound of sympathy—she'd only given Dean and Naomi the important details about her work history when they first interviewed her, but never divulged anything about her private life. It was a long time ago. How could Cat miss a mother she never knew?

"So, you're a loner? A drifter? No one to care about you, and no one to care about, either."

"I guess you could say that," Cat admitted from between clenched teeth. "But I can't see how that's relevant and I'm wondering what you're implying." He was painting a picture of her as if she was an unfeeling outsider. Which was untrue. She had plenty of feelings, she just kept a tight rein on them.

"He's not implying anything." Susan Nomad stepped in, casting her colleague a quick, quelling glance.

Deputy Nomad took over the questions from then on, of which there were plenty, testing Cat's patience to the limit. She could feel Levi willing her to hold onto her temper, and surprisingly, she did. He'd been right. Even if they weren't saying she was a suspect, they were beginning to wonder if she was involved. If she were somehow the target. Which was ridiculous.

Finally, Deputy Wilder told them that the arson investigation team were on their way down from the State Marshal's Office, and not to touch anything at the burned-out cabin until they'd inspected it.

The cops began to shuffle their papers together and wind

up the interview. Cat pushed her chair back, stood and stretched. Thank God, that was over.

She needed to get back to the machinery workshop. More than half of the day had been lost to Levi's bear and the fire.

"A word of caution, Ms. Lawson."

Cat turned around slowly to face Deputy Wilder. She lifted an eyebrow in his direction.

"Please don't leave town at the moment."

Her heart skipped a beat. Then the blood rose in her face. "What the hell is that supposed to mean?"

Levi grabbed her by the good arm. "Don't worry, Jude, I'll keep an eye on her." He tried to gently maneuver her out the door.

She wrenched her arm away from him. Who the hell did he think he was? No one was *keeping an eye on her*. Because she had nothing to hide. She had no intention of leaving. But the last thing she needed was a cop telling her not to. She would damn well leave town, if she wanted to.

CHAPTER NINE

Cat switched the motorcycle off and leaned it on the kickstand. The parking lot of the Montana Chocolate Company was nearly empty. Damn, she must've just missed closing time. She'd spent the past few hours trying to figure out what was wrong with Dean's small harvester, but found herself constantly being distracted by today's events. Finally, in a fit of exasperation, she'd thrown down her wrench and decided on a quick trip into town, to clear her head.

A scan of the door told her the closed sign was indeed hanging in the window. Goddammit, she'd been looking forward to stocking up on their chocolate. It was so good, it'd even appeared in her dreams. She'd have to buy some ordinary bars from the local Mini Mart, instead.

Cheap chocolate was better than no chocolate. So, she hopped off her motorcycle, removed her helmet and left it on the handlebar, then strolled down the sidewalk. The Mini Market was a little farther down Main Street, and she'd much rather shop there than at the Super 1 food shop out on the main highway. They should have everything she needed to re-stock with enough snacks to see her through the next few weeks. Emily had given her a list of items she wanted, as well. They were going to have a feast in their cabin tonight, tomorrow's sugar hangover be damned.

Low clouds hung over the mountains, blocking them from view. It was only a few minutes before six p.m. and the sun wasn't due to set for another half an hour, but the clouds were causing an early twilight. It cast an eerie pall over the quiet country town.

Cat couldn't wait until summer finally hit. Daylight saving would start in a month or so and the days would become longer and warmer. Almost balmy by most mountain men's reckoning.

Ten minutes later, she wandered back down the nearly empty pathway, only half concentrating on where she was going, her mind still muddling over the impudence of Deputy Wilder telling her to stay in town, and wondering what, if anything, the arson inspectors might've found at the burned-out cabin this afternoon.

But her mind wouldn't stay away from thoughts of Levi. Of their moment of madness in the bathroom earlier today.

After the interview with the cops, Levi had tried to get her to go and rest in her cabin. She'd told him exactly what she thought about that idea and stomped off toward the workshop, ignoring the way her arm throbbed painfully. He followed her, but she wouldn't turn around. She heard his loud exclamation of disgust as she dove into the familiar warmth of the workshop. He must've driven off soon afterwards, because half an hour later, when she emerged through the double doors, his truck was gone.

Perhaps she'd been a little harsh. She'd been angry. Angry at the deputies and their ridiculous questions. Angry at the person who was lighting fires on Dean's ranch. Angry at the world, really.

He'd told her he'd moved to a new rental property a few houses down from his previous one. She could ride past and check it out on her way home. He'd said she was welcome to come and meet Rekker anytime she wanted. Cat had never been up close to a raccoon before. Maybe she might even apologize.

Still lost in thought, she didn't immediately see the lone figure hovering over her bike.

"Hey," she said loudly. Her bike was the only vehicle in the small parking lot. She walked faster, her biker boots tapping loudly on the concrete.

When the guy heard her approaching, he lifted his hands as if to show he meant no harm, and smiled.

"I didn't touch anything, I promise," he said with another grin. "Just admiring her. She's a beauty." His gaze devoured the Triumph. He was an inch or so shorter than her, with sandy brown hair and a pleasant face. Wearing a pair of dark blue coveralls covered in grease stains, she could see his fingernails were lined with black.

"I'm Preston, by the way. I work down at the local auto shop." He extended a hand for her to shake.

"I'm Cat," she said, taking his hand.

"I was on my way home and spotted her. I've always wanted one of these babies," he said, a hint of jealousy evident in his voice.

Aha, the name Preston finally rang a bell. He must be the mechanic Dean she'd replaced. He seemed like a pleasant enough fellow, if perhaps a little unimaginative.

"If this beauty ever needs a service, bring her in, I'll take good care of her." He pointed across the road to where Cat guessed the auto shop was.

She nodded. "It's nice to meet you, Preston. But I need to get back to the ranch before dinner." She packed her stash of chocolate into the small pannier on the side and grabbed her helmet off the handlebar. "It was nice of you to offer to fix my bike, but I won't be needing your services. I'm a mechanic by trade, as well."

Preston's light-brown eyes took on a peculiar slant as he considered her words. She knew the moment he figured it out, because his eyes widened and he took a step back.

"So, I guess I'll be seeing you around." She lifted her foot over the back of the bike and settled herself on the seat.

"Oh, yeah, sure," he mumbled, taking a few more steps back.

"Take care." She gave him a wave as she turned the key and the bike roared into life. It was getting late, and she needed to get back to the ranch. It was important she not miss tonight's meal, as Dean and Naomi had promised all the staff an open and frank discussion about what was going on with the fires on the ranch. Cat hoped they might have some news from the arson investigation team by now, too.

As she hit the town limits, she opened up the throttle. The roar of her motorcycle, the way it leaped forward like an eager racehorse, had her whooping for joy. This was the life. Riding through country roads, the snow-capped mountains on either side pouring fresh, invigorating air into her lungs. The deciduous trees lining the road were beginning to sprout their new leaves, their spindly branches filling out, no longer looking skeletal against the evening sky. Soon, spring would be here in all its glory, turning everything green and lush.

It was dark by the time Cat pulled up beside her cabin. It was going to be cold tonight, and she was glad of her protective leathers keeping her warm on her ride back to the ranch. She quickly dumped her loot inside. Leaving her leather pants on, she changed her black jacket for her brand-new Stargazer coat Penny had sourced for her from the storeroom and headed for the lodge. If she was lucky, they may not have started dinner yet.

Opening the back door, she let the warmth and light from inside engulf her. Noise from the kitchen drifted down the hall, happy voices tangled together in conversation, welcoming her in. Joseph, the head chef, was overseeing the placement of large plates of food on the table, directing the two hired waitresses, Roxane and Janine where to put everything. Cat was surprised to see Roxy and Janine in the kitchen, they normally only worked the dinner shift, serving the guests before driving back into town. Dean must've asked them to stay behind to hear what he had to stay. Stella, the new chef's assistant was also there, standing at the back of the room, eyes big and wide as she regarded everyone. Big Tom sat next to Dale and the two men had their heads together in quiet conversation, but Cat still caught the prominent twang of Dale's Australian accent. She could see Steph's blonde hair in the corner; she was laughing at something Penny, the receptionist, had said. Cat found Emily's red hair amongst the throng of seated staff and noticed with relief that Emily had saved her a seat. Then her gaze fell on the person sitting on the other side of the empty seat, and she faltered.

Levi.

Her heart leapt inside her chest at the sight of him.

As if on cue, Levi turned his earthy gaze on her. "Evening," he said levelly, pulling the chair out so she could sit. "We thought you weren't going to make it."

She opened her mouth to ask him what he was doing here, but she already knew the answer. Dean must've invited him to join them. He was as much involved in this arson problem as the rest of them. Mainly due to her reckless actions. That thought spiked her displeasure. Why did he think he had to be her protector? Why had he followed her into that burning building?

"How's your arm?"

She swallowed the retort hovering on her lips. "It's good, thanks. Emily's going to help me to change the bandage tonight."

He'd followed her into the burning building because he was a good man, that was why. And she didn't deserve him.

Dean tapped his glass with his spoon until he had everyone's attention. "The police have questioned Mike Spencer, the guest who was staying here at the time of both the fires, and they're looking into his history. He wasn't happy at being a suspect, and wants to be moved into the Stevensville Motel, at least until the police have finished investigating him. Which is a shame, I think we've lost a loyal customer there." Dean sighed and dragged his hand through his hair. "I offered for him to stay here free of charge, but he wasn't very…"

"It's okay, Dean." Naomi's gaze softened as she looked at him. "I know how you hate to offend anyone. But he has a right to be angry."

"Yeah, especially if he's innocent," Dean replied with a frown.

"The police are just doing their job," Naomi countered quietly.

Cat looked around the table. Everyone had their eyes fixed on Dean and Naomi down at the far end. All of them looked worried, and Cat suddenly decided that rather than leave Dean with the dilemma of whether to tell the rest of the staff, she'd put him out of his misery.

"Just so you know," Cat interjected, "and for the sake of being completely open, the police also consider me to be a suspect."

There were gasps of surprise. Levi lay his hand on her back, lending his support.

"That's not strictly true," Dean said, loud enough to be heard over the general hubbub. "If anything, they think you're more of a target. But I just want you to know, we all have your back."

"Thank you, Dean. And Naomi. For your faith in me. I'd

never do anything to hurt this ranch."

"Of course, you wouldn't," Emily announced, patting Cat's hand. "But what about Clayton?" Emily asked the question on everyone's lips. "Surely, he's still their main suspect?"

"Yes. And no," Dean answered slowly. "No one has seen him for the last six months. He's got nothing in his past to indicate he'd do something like this. And the police want to follow up every line of enquiry."

"I can tell you the police have other people they are looking into," Naomi cut in. "But what I really want you all to take away from this, is that it isn't a cut-and-dried case. We need you to keep your eyes and ears open and consider all scenarios."

Cat understood what Naomi wasn't saying. Her underlying message. If it turned out that Clayton wasn't the arsonist, then the possibility was, it might be someone closer to home. Someone on the ranch.

"Dale, we also need you to stay vigilant." Dean's laser gaze zeroed in on his nephew. "The sheriff thinks that because you're family, you might also become a target."

Dale looked up, startled by Dean's words, as if he hadn't been paying full attention. "No probs, unc. I've got it covered."

Cat hid her smile at the young, brash cowboy's reply. He was only twenty-years-old and thought he was invincible. He was over here gaining experience working on the American ranch, hoping to take back some knowledge that might help when it came his turn to manage the large cattle station in Queensland.

"I need you to take this seriously, Dale. If you don't, your mom will make me send you home."

Dale sobered and sat a little straighter in his chair. "Yes, sir. I am. I am taking this seriously."

Dean speared him with a sharp gaze for a few more

seconds, before he brought his attention back to the rest of the staff. He conveyed the findings from the arson investigation team, while they ate. He told them what they already suspected. Accelerant had been used, and the fire had started at the front door. When Dean conveyed his gratitude no one had been harmed, one of the arson team mentioned that because of the timing of the fire—around midday—he believed the intention of the arsonist had been to make a statement, rather than hurt anyone. It was a pretty good guess that guests would either be at lunch at the lodge, or out taking part in one of the activities offered on the ranch. Which helped calm a few of Dean's anxieties.

The Ferguson family, whose cabin had burned down, had been moved up to the lodge, and Naomi had offered them a free return package, which Mr. Ferguson had gladly accepted, telling her there were no ill feelings. All their belongings had been incinerated, but insurance should cover that.

Naomi made sure the staff were all working in teams of two—to watch each other's backs at all times—and reassured everyone that if they felt unsafe on the ranch, to let them know.

Levi sat through it all without saying much, unless Dean asked him a specific question. But even though he barely spoke, Cat was acutely aware of him next to her. He seemed supremely comfortable sitting at the table with the staff. They all knew him and treated him like one of them. Emily had filled her in on the things she'd missed over the past six months, and she'd learned Levi had maintained his friendly contact with Dean and the rest of the staff. Even having one or two meals with them.

Cat watched Levi interact with Stella, the new cook from France, who'd only arrived a few weeks before Cat returned. Stella seemed a little on the shy side, and Cat hadn't gotten a chance to say more than a few words to her. Perhaps it was because Stella was still learning the language and found it hard when they all got talking so fast. Levi was warm and casual, putting her at ease with his cheerful grin. He was so candid, like an open book. The complete opposite to Cat.

Was the old saying true? Did opposites really attract? She didn't know. But watching him with Stella was causing a strange burning sensation in her chest. Which was stupid. Because Cat didn't get jealous. Ever. Eventually, she had to look away and began impatiently tapping her toe. When was this meeting going to end?

CHAPTER TEN

"It's okay, Levi, Emily's here. You don't need to play *knight in shining armor* tonight," Cat said as she exited the back door. She was pre-empting him, as if reading his mind. Because he'd been waiting for her outside to do just that. Make sure she got safely to her cabin. He also had something else on his mind.

He needed to talk to her about today. About their spontaneous sex session. He'd acted on the spur of the moment, but now he was left wondering. Wondering if she regretted it? If he regretted it?

Circumstances had thrown them together, and he'd been overcome by the emotion of the moment. But afterwards, it'd made him realize one thing. He was still in love with Cat. But she'd made it pretty clear she didn't want to have any more to do with him. Was that just part of her perfectly sculpted act of indifference and independence?

He'd noticed a change in Cat since she'd returned. That moment of vulnerability after the cabin fire, for one. She would never have allowed herself to show that kind of emotion before. And her commenting on how beautiful the mountains were. Admitting she'd missed this country.

Levi strolled over to where Cat, Emily, and Tom were

standing on the road. "I'd like to talk to you, if that's okay," he said quietly to Cat.

Not quietly enough, because Emily chimed in before Cat could even open her mouth. "You go with Levi, Tom can walk me to the cabin."

Levi sent her a silent thank you. "I'll make sure she gets back soon." He took Cat by the elbow and steered her away, around the side of the lodge as the other pair headed off up the hill.

Cat spluttered a few words of refusal, but when Levi didn't let go of her arm, she rolled her eyes and let him lead her. They walked in silence for a few seconds, the crunch of gravel under their boots the only sound.

Levi drew in a deep breath. "Cat, I..." He trailed off. Voices were coming from around the corner of the lodge, near a walkway to their right which led to a door into the dry storage area, where foodstuffs were kept for the kitchen. One of the voices suddenly rose in a panicked yell. What was going on? Levi and Cat exchanged a glance and they both turned and jogged towards the commotion. An orange glow beckoned them around the corner.

It was Stella, the new cook, and it looked to be one of the guests, both trying to beat out flames rising from the walkway, near the side entrance into the kitchen. Stella had a large tea towel and was stamping on the flames, and the man had taken his sweater off and was beating the fire out with that. It was small, as if it'd only just started. Or perhaps it hadn't been able to get a good hold on the damp wood of the walkway.

Stella turned around at the sound of their footsteps. "*Mon dieu*. Water. We need water," she yelled.

Cat dashed down a set of stairs that led farther into the garden, while Levi wondered where he could find a bucket to fill. But Cat was back sooner than he thought, turning a hose onto the flames. It didn't take long to douse them; Stella and the man had done most of the work already.

"*Sacre bleu,*" Stella said, panting a little as she took a step back. "If it was not for this man here, I might not have seen it." She swiped a hand across her brow.

Levi finally got a good look at the guest.

It was Mike Spencer.

The small hairs on the back of his neck stood to attention.

"Yes, I was walking back to my cabin, and I thought I saw something flickering. When I came to investigate, there was a figure crouching down near the walkway here." He pointed to the edge of the wooden platform. Was it Levi's imagination, or was the man speaking too quickly? "Whoever it was bolted when I called out, but by then the flames were already taking hold. So, I knocked on this door." He raised the same arm to indicate the side entrance. "And this young lady came out."

"Right." Levi watched the other man warily. He was under investigation for setting the cabin on fire. And now here he was, raising the alarm on another fire. The coincidence was too much. "I thought you were moving into the motel in town?" Levi tried to keep the censure out of his voice.

Mike shot him a guarded glance. "I decided to go first thing in the morning," he replied. "The hotel was booked solid tonight."

"Really?" Levi wasn't convinced.

"Hey, I know how this might look. But I had nothing to do with this." The man held his hands palm outwards, as if in surrender, and backed away.

Cat had been quietly watching the scene unfold as she turned the nozzle off and dropped the hose on the ground. "I'll go and find Dean. He'll need to sort this out."

"Good idea," Levi agreed. "I'll stay here and have a little chat with Mr. Spencer, until you get back." He hoped she also got the meaning hovering behind his words. For her to make sure Dean called the sheriff. Levi purposefully moved between Mike and the end of the walkway, blocking his escape. Cat hightailed it around the back of the lodge. Stella glanced between the two of them, obviously lost as to what was happening. She must not realize who this guest was.

"This is a whole load of bullshit." Mike clenched his fists at his sides.

Levi tensed, readying himself for whatever was to come. This guy was a lot older than him, in his late fifties, at least. Good-looking, tanned, wearing expensive jeans and shiny boots, he obviously kept himself in top condition. Could Levi take him down if he had to? Probably. Stella gasped and covered her mouth. She would be of no help. Should he send her back inside?

Suddenly the man unclenched his hands and dropped his shoulders. "I'm innocent. And I'll make sure the police know it." With that, Mike sat down on the edge of the walkway, away from the smoldering section and glared at him. Levi let out a silent breath.

The next two hours were spent with Dean and Deputy Wilder, giving an account of what happened, questioning Mike Spencer, and showing Jude the spot where the latest arson attack occurred.

Because there was no doubt in Levi's mind this was another arson attack.

Cat and Stella both told their stories and hovered in the background, as Deputy Wilder made sure he had all the facts. Jude decided he wasn't going to arrest Mr. Spencer, but he also agreed with Dean when he said perhaps Mr. Spencer should be escorted into town. Jude would find somewhere for Mike to stay, even if the motel was fully booked. By that stage, Cat and Stella said they were going to bed, if they were no longer needed, and both of them disappeared.

Levi helped Jude usher a still-fuming Mr. Spencer to the cruiser. It was late, after eleven, and he needed to get to bed, too. He should really jump in his truck and head home. But he wanted to check on Cat one last time. She said Emily would help her with her arm, but he wanted to take a look himself. It'd only take ten minutes, then he could head home and get some shuteye. It was damn cold outside, and Levi was looking forward to climbing into his truck and cranking up the heat. He also really needed to feed Rekker, who'd be most indignant to have gone without dinner for so long.

Rather than go through the lodge, Levi detoured around the outside, following a pathway that meandered through the gardens. Naomi had spent a lot of time and thought creating the garden. Said she wanted it to have that wild, spontaneous feel, as if someone were walking through a little bit of natural woodland. But it needed to have a feeling of order as well, without being heavy-handed about it, as if the trees and plants had always grown there. The pathway was illuminated with tiny solar lights that lit up the ground like fireflies. Naomi had commissioned a local sculptor to make life-size bronze statues of some of the native animals in the area. During the daytime, the kids—and adults alike—loved scurrying through the bushes discovering the half-hidden statues. And at night, the bronze figurines were expertly lit from below, so they seemed to come alive. A chipmunk on top of a rock. A large moose, complete with antlers, peering between two pine trees. A mother deer and her fawn grazing on the lawn in a hidden clearing. It was one more thing that made this place so special, and kept the guests coming back time and time again.

The garden path wandered out into a clearing at the back of the lodge and he turned right, up the gravel road leading to Cat's cabin. The roadway wasn't lit like the garden, and it was much harder to see. But he'd been this way many a time before, and the starlight was enough for him to make his way up the hill. His mind was still wandering among the shrubs and sculptures of the garden, so it took a few seconds for Levi to recognize there were voices up ahead. A male voice, kept low as if not wanting to be heard. And a female voice raised in an angry reply.

It was Cat's voice; he'd recognize it anywhere. But who was with her?

The sound was coming from a copse of small trees around fifty yards off the roadway. Was it Cat and Big Tom? But why would they be hiding out here, talking in the middle of the night?

Going on instinct, Levi slowed his pace, kept to the grassy spots and away from the gravel, where his footfalls could be heard. He wanted to find out what was going on before he announced himself.

Approaching the low-growing trees, he skirted around the perimeter, trying to find a way to see inside, without being spotted, himself.

Suddenly Cat's voice got louder. "Don't be a fucking idiot. You know you won't get away with this."

What was she talking about? And, more importantly, who was she talking to? Finally, he found a spot where he could peer in between the twisted branches and see the outline of two figures silhouetted by the stars in amongst the leaves. The shape on the right was definitely Cat. Levi could see her distinctive, spiked hair. But it was also the way she held herself, upright and defiant, hands on hips.

The other shape was harder to decipher. It wasn't Tom, not tall enough. But it was a man, in a bulky overcoat and knit hat.

Wait. Was the man holding a knife? Pointed straight at Cat's chest?

"Look, Clayton, this little plan of yours isn't going to work.

There's no way you're going to convince the sheriff you're innocent by keeping me as a hostage."

Holy fuck. It was Clayton. And he was holding Cat at knifepoint.

Levi couldn't think, all he could do was act. Cat was in danger. He rushed through the bushes to reach her.

CHAPTER ELEVEN

Cat wasn't quick enough. She took her eyes off Clayton and twisted around to see who was making the noise. Before she knew it, there was a knife at her throat. The blade was bone-chillingly cold and bit into her neck, paralyzing her in place. Then Clayton pinned her arm up behind her back, using her as a shield in front of him.

"Back off," Clayton shouted. "Whoever you are, just back the fuck off. I have a knife, and I won't hesitate to slit her throat."

The person crashing through the twisted branches came to a sudden halt around ten feet in front of them. She could hear him dragging in ragged breaths of air. Her heart was beating a million times a minute to the same rhythm as those gasping breaths.

Then a voice rang out, clear and strong in the cold night air. "Don't do anything stupid. I won't come any closer."

Levi. It was Levi.

A small part of Cat rejoiced somewhere deep in her head. Levi was here, he hadn't left her alone. Somehow, for whatever reason, he was here. Just like he'd been seven months ago, when he'd rescued her from the burning cabin. Just like he'd been today, when he'd also had her back. She'd been preparing to take Clayton on alone. There'd been no other choice, and she wasn't going to let him get away with kidnapping her. No way was she going anywhere with him, not willingly. Cat was used to fighting her own battles. Used to standing up for herself. The tough attitude wasn't all for show, there'd been times in her life when she'd stood up against much bigger, stronger opponents. Men who thought they could take advantage of a girl traveling on her own. So, she knew how to handle herself, had a brown belt in karate, and had taken many self-defense courses. But no man had ever held a knife to her throat before. She and Levi might stand more of a chance of talking Clayton down together.

In the time she'd been gone from the ranch, she'd managed to convince herself she didn't need Levi's help, that she was better off on her own. But right now, it was good to know she wouldn't have to do this unaided. Levi was here for her. It was something she never thought she'd ever admit. It was nice to know someone else had her back. Even if she never ended up needing him. In a blinding flash of light, it came to her; it was the fact he was there for her that mattered. Not the fact she was highly capable of doing everything on her own.

Clayton's last words made Cat wonder. Would he do what he was threatening? Did he have it in him to stab her in the neck? She didn't think so. But then was she prepared to stake her life on intuition alone?

"Tell me what you want, Clayton. Talk to me, so we can solve whatever problem it is you have." Levi's voice was calm, and she was impressed, under the circumstances. "Please don't hurt her."

"I won't, unless you make me," Clayton growled close to her ear.

Levi was an indistinct shadow in the darkness of the copse of trees. There was plenty of starlight; thankfully, the clouds from earlier had cleared. But very little light penetrated the thick branches. She could tell Levi had his hands raised in the air, showing Clayton he meant no harm. Pity he didn't still have his weapon strapped to his waist, but it'd be safely stowed in the lockbox in his car. He only wore that on occasions when he needed it, like tracking down an ornery old bear.

Cat was growing tired of Clayton's games. "Just tell him why you're here," she snapped. Clayton's grip on her arm tightened and she hid her whimper of pain, not wanting Levi to know she was hurting. At least it was her good arm he was twisting behind her back. She might well be screaming now, if it'd been her burned one.

"I'm innocent," Clayton declared, his breath hissing past her neck. "I didn't light those fires. I was set up."

Levi drew in a sharp breath, reacting in a similar way to how she had when she'd first heard Clayton's declaration. Why in hell Clayton thought they were going to believe him was beyond her. He was guilty as hell, as far as she was concerned.

"Okay," Levi said slowly. "So why did you run? Why didn't you stay and tell the police that seven months ago?" Levi was asking the same questions she'd already asked. They were going over and over the same ground.

"Because I knew they wouldn't believe me."

Well, duh. Cat managed to swallow her snort of derision.

"And why should they believe you now?" Levi asked, calm and sure.

"Because I'm tired of living life on the run. I've come back to clear my name. You have to know it wasn't me that night in your house. Someone stole my truck. It had my Stargazer coat and hat in it."

This was new. Clayton hadn't gotten to that part yet, he'd been so busy telling her he wasn't guilty, but he hadn't said why. Levi hesitated, the words coming as a shock to him, too.

"Whoever that person was in your house, they were wearing my clothes, and driving my truck, but it wasn't me."

"So, who was it then, Clayton?" Levi was keeping his voice under control, hands up in the air, but Cat could sense his mind was going a million miles a minute, trying to figure out if any of Clayton's wild tale could be true.

"I don't know, otherwise I would've told you." Clayton's grip released a little on her arm, more intent on getting them to believe him than on making sure she stayed captive. "Did the cops ever find any fingerprints? Any other forensic evidence I was there?"

"No, but the sheriff said you could have been wearing gloves," Levi countered quickly.

"It's your word against mine, then," Clayton said, removing the knife from her throat to point it at Levi, seeming to forget he was holding her prisoner. "I really need you to remember. Think back to that night. You must've seen the guy's face. At least caught a glimpse of him. If you saw he was wearing my clothes, then you must've been close enough to see his face." Clayton's voice rose a few octaves. His grip loosened some more, so intent was he on getting through to Levi.

"I don't..." Levi hesitated, then seemed to change his mind. "On the other hand...now I think about it...maybe you're on to something." Levi slowly brought a hand up to scratch his beard, as if in deep thought. Good idea, distract Clayton, get him thinking they believed him. Soften him up so he dropped his defenses. Because there was no way Cat wanted to stay here listening to Clayton spout nonsense all night.

Cat made a sudden decision. It was now or never. Levi was still talking, but Cat tuned him out, going through her options on the best way to break Clayton's hold. His left hand was still pinning her arm behind her back, but it'd loosened considerably. His right hand held the knife, waving it around in the air in front of her. Which meant her right arm was free, as were her feet. There were a couple of tactics she could use to break free, but the knife made them a little trickier to execute.

Clayton was a large man, who towered above her, and he had a big weight advantage. Once she'd taken him by surprise, she was counting on Levi's help to get him under control.

She waited until Levi finished speaking and Clayton began to say something in reply. With all her might, she swung her hand back and down. There was a satisfying thud as she connected with his crotch and he uttered a loud *Oof.* Just as she hoped, he stepped back and bent over, as most men who've been hit in the balls do. Without hesitation, Cat then brought her same arm up and whipped it backward, straight into the side of Clayton's face. It hurt her arm, but she ignored it as Clayton fell to the ground in a heap. Cat was on top of him in a second, trying to restrain him.

"Get the knife," she screamed at Levi, who was already shoving his way through the shrubbery toward them. Clayton struggled beneath her as she sat astride him, turning on his back and pushing her away with one arm, the knife arcing toward her. The metal blade glinted in the starlight, and Cat made ready to fend him off with her forearm. She sucked in her breath and braced. But the slice of the blade never came. Levi's boot landed on Clayton's wrist just as his fist collided with the struggling man's face.

"Leave her alone, asshole," Levi shouted. But Clayton didn't hear him, because his eyes had already rolled back in his head. Levi's punch knocked him out cold.

Cat stood quickly, in a hurry to get away from the loathsome man. Levi bent down to get a better look at him, then once he was convinced Clayton wasn't getting up anytime soon, he picked up the knife off the ground and came to stand next to Cat.

"Thanks." She was still trying to catch her breath. "If you hadn't been so quick off the mark, he might have got me."

"I was half-expecting you to do something crazy," Levi replied. "So, I was ready for just about anything." Even in the dark, Cat could tell he was giving her one of those looks. The one filled with exasperation, left eyebrow raised, whenever she did something he couldn't quite believe. She shrugged. She couldn't help it if she sometimes reacted before she thought something through properly. Yes, some people might consider it a flaw, but it was the way she did things. At least Levi knew her well enough to predict what she was about to do. Which was a slightly scary thought, because it meant he knew her better than most people.

Levi moved so quickly Cat didn't have time to react. He pulled her into his arms, held her tight against his chest. Strong biceps, solid and sure, wrapped around her. "God, Cat," he said. "If I'd been a second later, he might've got you with that knife."

"I know," she replied, only half-focused on his words, enjoying the smell of quintessential Levi as he held her, and she buried her nose in his neck.

"I could've lost you tonight." His words were quiet, but they penetrated the nice buzz she had going, and all those thoughts about kissing him on the neck evaporated. "I don't know what I'd do if I lost you."

Cat pulled back, wanting to look him in the eyes. But it was so dark, she could only make out the shadows of his face. "I'm fine," she said lightly. "I had a plan. I was going to fend him off. Protect myself until you got there."

There was a glint as his eyes caught a hint of starshine. "You always have to push it to the upmost limits, don't you?" Levi sighed.

"What else did you expect me to do? Wait until he had us both hog-tied and bundled us into his getaway car? Kidnapped us?" She stepped back, out of his embrace and glanced down at Clayton. Still out cold. She ran a hand though her hair. "You keep wanting to protect me, Levi. But I'm not some fragile woman who needs a man to guide her every step of the way."

"I know that, Cat," he replied. "Believe me, I do. It's just that..." He hesitated, lifting his gaze to the sky. "It's almost like you're so fearless, so determined. Like you have a death wish, sometimes. And it scares me."

She snorted. He was wrong. The words, *I don't have a death wish*, hovered on her tongue. But a tiny kernel of doubt kept her mouth firmly shut.

It was time to change the subject; this debate was going nowhere, and they still had to take care of Clayton. "I'll get Deputy Wilder on the line. He won't be happy about coming back here tonight." She reached for her phone in her coat pocket, hiding the fact she was nursing her burned arm. She'd take a look at it later, in the privacy of her bathroom.

"I'll keep an eye on Clayton." Levi didn't look at her as she went to call the deputy. Now that the danger was over, she could feel the cold night settling in, making her shiver.

Why did everything always come down to a fight between them? Why couldn't Levi just accept her for who she was?

CHAPTER TWELVE

Levi tossed a piece of fruit in the air and watched Rekker catch it neatly in his front paws. It was mid-morning and he was sitting on his back porch, staring at the mountains looming behind the fence. A hint of green, spring growth was starting to color the lower foothills, buds bursting on the oaks and birch trees, softening the scenery, so the fir trees no longer looked stark against the light-blue sky.

Last night felt like a bit of a dream already, but head office had given Levi a few days off, to recover from *his encounter with the arsonist.* Their words, not his. Normally, Levi would've refused their offer. He preferred to be busy; he loved his job. But he had no energy today, like he couldn't find the motivation to do much of anything. He hoped he was allowed back to work shortly, he wanted to be involved in the relocation of the rogue bear from the Stargazer Ranch property, which should happen soon. They'd organized a team, headed by Ranger Woodhouse from the Missoula Office, who specialized in large animal capture. He'd bring the tranquilizer guns and a large cage, so they could load the animal and take it to the WILD rehabilitation center. It was due to take place the at the end of the week, and Levi wanted to make sure he was part of the team.

The raccoon made a purring noise and stood on his hind legs, which meant he really enjoyed that morsel of food, and could he please have some more. Levi smiled and tossed him another piece of apple. It was nice to have a companion, even if it was a rascally little native critter with a mind of its own. It made the house a little less lonely. Not that Levi minded living on his own. After all, it'd been a dream of his growing up on the reservation to get away from living under his father's thumb. And out from living in his brother's shadow. To be able to afford to rent a house he could call his own.

Thinking about his family made him idly wonder how they were doing. His father, Sahale considered himself an important man within the Bitterroot Salish tribe. But the truth was a little less grandiose. Sahale had tried many times to be elected to the Flathead Reserve Tribal Council but had failed in every bid. The sad fact was everyone knew Sahale was a drunk. His father believed he'd done a good job of bringing up his two boys, teaching them the old ways, making sure they stayed true to their culture. But Levi's version was a lot less impressive. Sure, Levi and his older brother, Wyatt, had been shown the traditional ways of hunting, fishing, and living off the land. But their lessons had ended abruptly when Levi was eleven years old. The day his mother left. Why a feisty Italian woman had ever agreed to marry his father was beyond Levi. Looking back now, Levi was surprised she'd lasted that long. Sahale had taken her leaving extremely hard. That was the day Wyatt had started down his own dark path, as well.

Levi wondered how much longer Wyatt had to go on his jail sentence. A stab of self-reproach flushed through his belly. He really should go and visit his brother. But he had no idea what he'd say to him.

The distinctive sound of a motorcycle broke the quiet morning air. Levi shook off his dark thoughts and stood. It could mean only one thing. Levi's stupid heart did a somersault in his chest, and he tamped down the feeling. Just because Cat was here, there was no need for his blood to fizz through his veins. They'd probably end up fighting again, anyway.

Rekker followed him down the hall to the front door. He was barefoot, wearing old sweatpants and an even older blue shirt that he'd wear to fix his truck in. But there was no time to change, because he could see Cat's shadow appear on his front porch, through the small glass window.

He opened the door. Cat stood there, wearing her black leathers, blonde hair mussed from the helmet and cool, blue eyes that seemed to look right through him. Long, trim legs went all the way down to motorcycle boots. She really rocked the biker chic look. Jesus, why did she have to look so good? His body reacted, just like it always did, his cock hardening.

"I thought it was you. Come in," he said, turning slightly away to hide the growing bulge in his pants. How was he ever going to get her out of his system if his cock did whatever it wanted as soon as she appeared on the scene?

"Oh, my God. That is the cutest thing I've ever seen." Levi never thought he'd hear Cat sound as much like a gooey teenage girl as she did right in that moment. Cat bent down and peered between Levi's legs. What the hell…? But it wasn't Levi Cat was interested in, it was his raccoon.

Rekker gave a friendly chitter and then—much to Levi's surprise—came forward and stood on his hind legs, reaching his front paws up toward Cat.

"You can pet him, but I definitely wouldn't pick him up," Levi warned. Even though that was exactly what it looked like Rekker was asking for. Little traitor. He was shy around most other people. Trust the critter to take to Cat straight away.

Cat cooed at Rekker as he frolicked down the hall after

them.

"I'd offer you a beer, but it's not even midday yet." Levi leaned against the far kitchen counter, watching Cat as she played with the raccoon. Finally, she stood and faced him.

"Sorry, I didn't mean to barge in. I wasn't even sure if you'd be home, given it's a Monday."

"No probs." He waved off her excuses.

Her blue eyes bored into him, as if she were unsure of something. Him perhaps. Which was a first. She broke her stare and said, "I've just come from the sheriff's office. Dean and I went to see what's happening with Clayton."

He stood up straighter. "And?"

"He's still professing his innocence. Very loudly, and to whomever will listen."

"Well, all the evidence is pointing towards him at the moment. And trying to kidnap you to prove his point won't help his case one little bit. I hope they prove him guilty, and he spends a long time locked up."

Cat chewed her lip and wouldn't look at him.

"What's the matter?" He took two steps across the kitchen so he could stand directly in front of her.

"Nothing. Not really. The sheriff seemed to think the same thing. He's got his man and now the case is closed."

"And that's a great thing," Levi stated. "It means we can all finally relax around here."

Cat pursed her lips and nodded. There was something she wasn't saying.

"But?" he asked.

Her gaze came back to meet his and she stared, blue eyes wide, as if considering her next words carefully. "Did you get the feeling that Clayton might've been telling the truth last night? He did seem pretty desperate. And you admitted that you never got a good look at his face the night he set fire to your house."

"You surely can't be considering any of that bullshit he spouted? It was him. It had to be him that night." But even more importantly, Clayton had put Cat's life at risk. The man needed to be locked away. He enunciated his next words very clearly. "He. Was. Going. To. Kill. You."

"I know, I know," she said, looking down at her boots.

He took her by the shoulders. "What's going on with you? The old Cat would've been happy for this guy to rot in jail for the rest of his life. Clayton is a deadbeat. An arsonist."

"What do you mean, the old Cat?" She tensed beneath his hands, but didn't withdraw completely, instead, watching him warily. Trust her to zero in on those few words that'd slipped out before he could stop them.

He wasn't really sure what he meant. This was probably going to cause another argument, but it needed to be said. "Something about you has changed since I saw you last." She wouldn't want to hear that he saw a softer side in her. How could he put it, so she didn't turn into a little hellcat, like she normally did? "Changed for the better," he clarified.

"Like what?"

For a few seconds he'd forgotten how close he was standing to her. But now she was looking at him, that angelic face tipped up, serious mouth in a slight pout as she waited on his reply.

"You seem more open… More willing to…" God, this was hard to articulate. "Listen to what other people have to say."

Cat frowned and pursed her lips. Did she understand what he was trying to express? Or was she a volcano, bubbling hot lava underneath and about to erupt?

He plowed on, regardless. "Like yesterday, when we stopped to appreciate the mountains. And you said you missed this place."

Her gaze flicked to his and then away.

"The old Cat would never have admitted that."

There was a deathly silence as she considered his words. Should he also mention those few fleeting seconds in her cabin, when she'd let him look after her, had been desperate to make love with him?

Before he could phrase the words, she broke the silence. "Maybe not." Sudden confusion flooded her face. At the same time, she shrugged, and he realized he was still holding her by the shoulders. "Yeah, I guess it's one of the reasons I came back. Because I missed it here."

"What about me? Did you miss me?" Levi wasn't sure he was ready for her answer, but it was too late now, he couldn't take back the words. She started, and tried to back away, but he was holding onto her, and she had nowhere to go.

Shaking her head, she glared up at him. Opened her mouth and closed it again. He waited for the word *no* to pass her lips. Waited for her to deny emphatically that she never needed or wanted him. She'd always been so determined she didn't need any man, and hadn't been shy about telling him so. Back then, Levi had been under the illusion he could change Cat, that he could induce her to break down those walls around her heart and she'd eventually fall in love with him. He couldn't have been more mistaken. Because all his efforts had failed, and all he'd done was succeed in driving her away.

Back then, she hadn't been ready to let anyone else into her heart. And he'd been too blind to see it. But now…? How much had she really changed inside? And how far did he dare push it? Was he really prepared to go there again with her?

"Did you miss me, Cat?" he whispered slowly once more.

She glared at him and her hands came up to rest on his chest, to push him away. But instead of pushing, her fingers tightened on the fabric of his shirt, taking a big fistful in each hand. Then she did something totally unexpected, she dragged him toward her. His lips were on hers before he knew what was happening, her tongue diving into his mouth, needy and hot. The same as the other day, his blood roared strong and fast through his veins. Their chemistry was undeniable. He turned them both, letting his hips rest against hers as he pushed her up against the countertop. The feel of her butt through the leather pants as he brought his hands up to cup her ass was amazing. The fabric hugged her legs like a second skin.

"Can I take that as a yes?" he said when she finally broke the kiss, panting and staring at him, wide-eyed.

"You can take it however you want, Mr. Wilson." Her tone was dark and low, but her eyes glittered dangerously, the blazing bright blue of a flame in a gas burner. Licking her lips, she gave him a slow, sexy smile, inviting him in. Goddammit, he was in trouble. The kind of trouble that might have him losing his heart all over again.

CHAPTER THIRTEEN

It was Levi's raccoon that finally brought Cat to her senses. Tiny claws scrabbled at her leg as he made a nervous chittering sound. Levi seemed to hear it at the same time, because he was the one to break their kiss. He looked down and gave a grunt of frustration.

His gaze found hers and held it. "Sorry about that. He's never seen me kissing a woman before, he probably thinks you're attacking me." He attempted a smile, but it faded when she didn't join in. Her body felt boneless, as if he'd taken away her will to move. She was finding it hard to regain her equilibrium after that scorching kiss.

Her only aim in coming here this morning had been to tell Levi about Clayton. They should both be rejoicing that he was now behind bars. Like Levi said earlier, they were free of fear, now. There'd be no more fires at Stargazer Ranch. She'd wanted to celebrate with him because he, of all people, would understand. Instead, she found herself wondering at Clayton's stubborn refusal to admit he was guilty. It'd clouded her happiness at being able to count her blessings with Levi. And instead, she wanted Levi to convince her she was crazy. And look where that'd led. She'd let down her defenses. For the second time, if you wanted to count their bathroom tryst.

Was he right? Had she changed from the woman he used to know? It'd only been six months, surely people didn't alter drastically in that small amount of time? But then again, perhaps it hadn't been a monumental shift in Cat's values. Perhaps it was one of those small changes, the kind you don't see coming until it's too late.

She should go. Dean was expecting her back at the ranch, and she hadn't intended on staying even this long. But her arms wouldn't push Levi away. They wanted to pull him in close again. She had missed him. It was time she admitted that to herself, if not to Levi. Dean's call, asking her to come back to the ranch had been a convenient excuse, but deep down, she knew she would've found her way back eventually.

What she was going to do with that information was a whole other question. One she would not be answering right now. Not when Levi's arms were still draped around her waist, the feel of his beard scratching her face still reverberating inside her. She liked his beard. It tickled the sensitive places at the corners of her mouth.

Even though she needed to get going, her body wanted to stay. It wanted a replay of the sex scene yesterday, and her thighs clenched convulsively at the thought. But that wasn't why she'd come here today. She needed to get her cravings under control. Needed to go and figure out why Levi had such an effect on her. What it all meant.

"I'd better go. I don't want to upset Rekker." She smiled down at the little, masked face, staring up at them intently. "It's cute he's so protective of you."

"Yeah," he muttered, not releasing her. "Real cute." He obviously wasn't going to be the one to break their embrace. Dark eyes were still fixed intently on her, full of deep emotions. And hunger. Levi wanted her. He had the same look in his eyes as he'd had yesterday. When she'd let him take her. Let their passion overflow. It'd be so easy to do it again today. Let him take her to his bed. Make love to him, like she yearned to do.

Reaching somewhere deep inside, she found the strength to push him gently away.

"I've got lots to do back at the ranch. Dean's going to start sowing his sorghum soon, and the seeder needs fixing."

He finally got the message and stepped back, disentangling his arms from hers and allowing her to move sideways along the countertop, away from him. Those dark, sepia eyes shuttered, hiding whatever emotions he was feeling from her once more. Hiding the disappointment.

"Why aren't you at work?" she asked, suddenly aware that this was Monday.

Levi lowered his eyebrows and stroked an irritated hand over his beard. "The director of human resources thought it might be a good idea if I took a few days off. I have to go and see a psych up in Missoula tomorrow as well, can you believe it?"

Cat paused. Maybe seeing a psych wasn't such a bad idea. Dean had asked her something similar this morning, but she'd brushed him off with one of her usual quelling looks. Said she'd think about it. She felt fine. But Levi had a gentler soul than her, it might do him good to talk about last night with someone who was unbiased and calm.

"Yeah, shitty HR people, always having to tick those shitty boxes." She nodded in agreement. "But I guess it's easier to get it over and done with, rather than fight them on it."

Levi gave her an odd look, like he could hardly believe those words had come out of her mouth. "You may be right. Who knows, I might even pop over and see Wyatt while I'm in town."

Cat lifted her chin to stare at him. That's right, she'd almost forgotten Levi's brother, Wyatt, had been in jail when they were dating six months ago. Cat couldn't remember how much longer he had to serve on his sentence. Levi didn't normally like to talk about it, and she hadn't wanted to pry. It surprised her to hear him mention his brother.

"That's a good idea," she agreed. "He is family, after all."

Levi scowled and Cat thought she might've hit a nerve. She didn't even know the reason Wyatt was in jail. Perhaps he was a complete deadbeat, he could even be murderer. But knowing Levi, she found it hard to believe a brother of his could turn out that awful.

"Speaking of family, have you seen your father recently?" he asked.

Cat stiffened. Levi knew she hated talking about her father, Robert. Was he trying to get back at her for her comment about family? She had valid reasons for not wanting to discuss her father. Their relationship was complicated. Cat didn't remember her mother, not really. She'd died when Cat was two years old, and her father had raised her after that. He'd done the best job he could; the best job he was capable of. He'd taught Cat everything she knew about being a mechanic, and that counted for a lot. If only he could stay away from the booze. Her father was a different man when he wasn't drinking, talkative and easygoing. But those times were few and far between. In the end, Cat had to get away, especially when he'd started using his fists instead of words.

"Nope. I heard Robert was working down in Utah, in a little place called Provo. I thought of going to see him after my job in Vegas finished. But then Dean called, and, well, here I am." She waved her good arm in a flourish. Her burned arm hurt if she moved it quickly, but she managed to hide her grimace. In all the uproar last night, Levi hadn't checked it for her, like he'd promised to do. She was surprised he hadn't asked her about it today.

Bryan was an old boss of her father's and he kept tabs on him for her. She'd contact Bryan whenever the guilt got too bad, and he'd give her the latest update. Bryan always worried about young Cat, while having a soft spot for Robert. They'd worked for Bryan for nearly a year. The longest they'd ever stayed anywhere. Her gypsy lifestyle had come from living with her father. Working as a mobile mechanic, often straight out of his truck, he was constantly on the move from town to town, state to state, towing their large mobile home behind him. Sometimes an auto shop would give him a few months' work and they'd settle for a while. But then, as he put it, his feet would start to itch, and they'd be on the move again.

She'd never told Levi about the many times her father had become violent as she got older. He never hit her when she was young, but after she'd turned fourteen, he'd started looking at her differently. The words, *you look so much like your mother*, had only left his mouth on a single occasion, but they remained burned into Cat's memory, enough for her to know he was fighting his own internal demons and her staying only made them worse. Only one other person really knew what her life had been like living with Robert, and that was Bryan.

Levi had never spoken to her about growing up on the reservation, either. Apart from saying once that he wished his father would go to AA and find a solution to his problem. Admittedly, they'd only been together a month, and had other things on their mind whenever they managed to find time together back then. Perhaps they were more alike than either of them imagined. Both of their fathers were drunkards. How ironic.

Regardless of that fact, it was time for Cat to get out of Levi's house. She bent down and gave Rekker another pet between the ears. Such a sweet critter. Who knew they could be so endearing?

"I really have to get going." She made her way down the hall, Levi a few steps behind, his bare feet making hardly any sound on the wooden floorboards.

"Does that mean the sheriff is letting Mike Spencer off the hook?" Levi's question took her by surprise, and Cat swiveled as she got to the front door.

"Yes, Sheriff Buchanan told us Mike was free to leave the area. The sheriff has finally confirmed he's got a solid alibi for the cabin fire yesterday morning. Mike said he was birdwatching over at Lake Como yesterday morning, and Deputy Wilder finally tracked down an older couple who spent some time with him strolling along the Loop Trail. The poor guy just wants to go home and forget about all this. Can you imagine, having the police suspect you of arson, and the whole time you're completely innocent?"

"Hmm." Levi was looking at the floor. A strand of hair had escaped from the tie at the nape of his neck and she had a sudden urge to tug it all free, she liked it when his hair hung down around his face. But then, she hadn't seen it down since she'd been back, maybe it'd look different with the beard. She turned and opened the door.

"I like your new house, by the way," she said. It was old and in need of some work, a wooden, two-story house, with high gables and a cute little front porch. A coat of paint would brighten up the white exterior, but the large front yard was neat and tidy. The little she'd seen of the interior she'd liked, as well. It had character, felt welcoming, with the warmth of the wooden floorboards, the high ceilings finished with decorative molding; the large, open fireplace she'd spotted in the living room. It'd be a nice place to come home to. Cozy.

Whoa, where had that come from? She'd never thought of any one place as being home before. Her life was on the move.

"They still haven't rebuilt the one that burned down." Levi indicated with his chin down the road, where his old rental had been. The one Clayton had set fire to and tried to murder Levi at the same time. "They bulldozed the remnants of the old place, but I think the owners are still haggling with insurance. Shame really, it's like looking at a scar on the landscape every time I drive down the road." Cat could imagine it'd be a powerful reminder to Levi, seeing the place where he could so easily have died. Levi had a lot more reasons to hate Clayton than she did. She couldn't fault him for not believing Clayton when he professed his innocence. Why then, did that annoying voice still niggle at the back of her mind?

"I hope they build a new one soon," she replied, taking the steps off the front porch two at a time.

"See you around, Cat." His voice echoed behind her.

"Yeah, see ya." She didn't look back. Couldn't look back. Walked down the gravel driveway, unsure of when she'd see him next. So many things hung in the air between them, unsaid. How were they ever going to move on? Cat knew she needed to make a decision but had no idea where to start.

"Cat, wait a minute." Levi's voice stopped her in her tracks. "We need to—"

"Sorry, Levi. I've got to get back to work." She straddled her motorcycle and pulled on her helmet. It was like there was a magnet in her chest, pulling her back toward him. She had to leave now, or she might never go.

Her bike roared to life and she took off down his driveway, not looking back.

CHAPTER FOUTEEN

Levi yawned and lay his head back against the driver seat as he turned off the truck. Spring had hit with a vengeance. The past few days had been unseasonable warm and today was almost balmy. He stared up at the watercolor-blue sky overhead. Now that he'd turned off the engine, birdsong wafted in through his open window. These were the days he lived for. It was his first day back at work after his enforced leave, but even three days off had him itching to get back on the job. He was on his way back from checking on the campers at Painted Rocks State Park, and he'd pulled over for a much-needed coffee. It'd been a long morning and the hot thermos of coffee he always kept stocked up in his truck was beckoning. Rekker continued to wake him before dawn every morning. He was going to have to do something about that critter. All the advice was not to let a pet raccoon sleep inside, but Levi might have to try it. At least if Rekker was already inside, he wouldn't wake the whole neighborhood with his cries.

Thinking about the raccoon, Levi's thoughts drifted back to Monday morning, when Cat had stopped by to see him. And her reaction to Rekker. She'd clearly fallen in love with the animal. There were so many things he'd wanted to say to her that day. They had unfinished business. And Clayton had been a part of that. While he'd been at large, they had a shared enemy, a shared fear he might come back and finish what he started. But now Clayton was no longer a threat, that bond no longer held them together.

Watching her walk down his driveway, away from him, he'd been hit with a sudden feeling he was losing her. If he let her get on her bike and ride away, he might never see her again. As she sat astride her motorcycle, he'd even called out, meaning to make her stay. Wanting to hold her in his arms again, spend a lazy day together in bed. Or not so lazy, if the mood took them. But Cat had started her motorcycle and let the roar of the engine drown out anything else he said. He'd watched as she guided the bike effortlessly down the road and turned the corner.

He'd kicked himself later that he'd forgotten to ask how her burned arm was doing. But she didn't seem to be favoring it, which must be a good sign.

It was partly because of Cat's endorsement that Levi had gone to see Wyatt. After steeling himself to walk through those barred gates—he'd almost turned around more than once—he was glad he'd made the trip. Wyatt was so pleased to see him, he talked non-stop about his plans for the future. He would be released in less than two months, and he couldn't wait to get out. It might've been a stupid thing to do, but on the spur of the moment, Levi offered Wyatt a place to stay, if he needed it.

The two-way radio crackled to life, snapping him away from his thoughts.

"Ranger Wilson, respond. Are you there, Ranger Wilson?"

Levi smiled at the professional tone coming from the radio. Ranger headquarters' dispatcher, Thelma, always sounded so businesslike and cool on the radio, when in reality she was the life of the station, always cracking jokes, with a welcoming grin on her face. A general all-round nice woman.

"Wilson here, reading you. How are you this morning, Thelma?"

"Morning, Levi." She didn't enter into chit-chat, remained efficient and calm. "Got a call two minutes ago. Smoke spotted up near Romney Ridge. Not sure if it's a hoax. Can you go and check it out?"

A frisson of ice ran down Levi's spine. Was he always going to react this way whenever fire reared its ugly head in Bitterroot Valley? But this fire—if it even was a real fire— wasn't at Stargazer Ranch. It was close, but it was in the state forest, not on their land, so there was no need to worry. And Clayton was locked up tighter than a bug's ass in jail. So, there was no more threat from that particular arsonist.

"I'm on my way. Will let you know what I find." Levi replaced the mouthpiece into the cradle. But before he started the truck, he grabbed the pair of binoculars he always had stashed behind his seat and climbed into the bed of the truck. From his vantage point, it took him a few seconds to pinpoint the correct ridgeline, but when he did, there it was. A thin wisp of smoke washing into the blue sky.

Shit.

It looked like the real thing.

Had someone left a campfire unattended? There were hikers all through these mountains. But it was a little early in the season for most of them, yet. The nights often dipped near freezing, so a hiker would have to be well-equipped and committed to plan a trip right now. Perhaps the warmer weather was tricking people into coming out before time.

The area was fairly remote. Levi racked his brain, trying to remember if there were any roads or firebreaks running that far into the mountains. Canyon Creek Trailhead started at the bottom of the ridge. During summer, hikers used the trail to get to the top of Canyon Peak all the time. But for him, it was probably best to access the area though Stargazer Ranch; they had trails for horse riding, mountain bikes and their four-wheelers carved all the way across that forest.

He jumped back into his truck, ignoring the way his heart rate quickened at the thought of going to Stargazer. This had nothing to do with Cat. He probably wouldn't even see her. And after the way she left the other day, he wasn't sure what kind of reception he might receive.

Levi hit the road and punched some numbers on his cell, sitting in a cradle on the dash. When Penny, the receptionist at Stargazer Ranch answered, he told her to warn Dean he was on his way and asked if he could borrow a four-wheeler to get up into the mountains to check out the fire.

The ranch was only ten minutes up the road; it was lucky he was on his way back from Painted Rocks and not at the other end of the valley, or he could have been hours away, not merely minutes.

He could see the curl of smoke clearly now, and it was getting bigger. Not bothering to stop at the main parking lot, Levi drove straight past the lodge and up to the machinery workshop, hoping Dean was already there, waiting for him. His gaze searched the inside of the building, even as he leaped out of his truck, looking for the familiar, lithe figure of Cat bent over one of her beloved pieces of equipment. He couldn't see her. Unless she was hiding underneath a tractor, or in the small break room tucked away in the corner.

The large shape of a man loomed at the side of the shed, near the four-wheelers.

"Tom, is that you?" Levi strode toward the big man.

"Hi, Levi. Dean asked me to get a couple of quads ready. I'm going with you." Big Tom grimaced quickly in Levi's direction and went back to strapping something on the rear of one of the quads.

"Okay." Levi didn't need help, but he wasn't going to

argue. All that was required of him was to pinpoint the fire's location and alert the fire services on the best way to tackle it. If possible, he could try putting the fire out himself. But by the look of that smoke, it'd already be too big. "Where's Ca —?"

"Great, you're here." Dean marched through the large, double doors, and Levi closed his mouth.

"Thanks for loaning me a quad. And Tom."

"Not a problem. That fire looks like it's either near the edge of my property, or in the state forest, but either way, it's still too damn close for comfort. Tom's got all the equipment you should need, including a hand-held GPS, and some flares, as well a couple of two-ways and a satellite phone. You guys need to hurry if you're going to find Cat."

Levi froze. What had Dean said? The confused look on his face must've said it all, because Dean asked, "Didn't Tom tell you?"

"Tell me what?"

"Cat is up there with a couple of guests from the ranch. She took them on a mountain bike tour up to Canyon Peak. Dale was supposed to take them, but he's come down with the stomach flu. And you know how reception is patchy up there. I'm having trouble getting hold of her. We need to find them and bring them down."

Shit. Cat was on the mountain, in the thick of danger. As usual. Along with two of Dean's guests. This changed things. Was it just another coincidence? Cat being directly affected by yet another fire. He didn't have time to puzzle that one out.

"I've got to quickly call this into HQ. I'll get them to put search and rescue on standby, as well as the fire department." Levi jogged over to his truck.

Two minutes later, he returned with a frown on his face.

"What's up?" Tom asked.

"I just talked to dispatch. Thelma has put the local fire

department on notice. But…"

"But what?" Tom prompted.

"There's an emergency up at Kootenai Canyon. There've been reports of the possible death of a climber, and another couple of climbers stuck half-way up a cliff-face. Missoula search and rescue on their way up there as we speak."

"That's not good." Tom said, rubbing his chin.

"No, it's not," he replied with a grimace. Because it meant he and Tom were on their own if it came to an emergency rescue. He followed Tom out of the shed on his four-wheeler.

"I'll keep trying to get hold of Cat," Dean yelled over the engines, then touched the brim of his hat and waved them off.

They headed directly north, straight across the pastures, in a different direction than the one he and Cat had taken to find the rogue bear. Which was one tiny relief; at least the injured bear wasn't under threat from the fires. If only they'd finished the relocation earlier. But it was too late to worry about it now. They were going too fast for him to talk to Tom, but there was really no need. They both knew what they needed to do and where they needed to be. Fast.

It took them ten minutes, cutting through the pastures and dodging a few startled cattle, to reach the boundary fence separating the grassland from the low foothills of the mountains. Big Tom slowed his quad and turned left, following the wooden railings. Levi had a vague idea where to look for the gate that'd let them through, but he was glad Tom was here, as he knew exactly where it was and saved him precious minutes of searching.

Both of them looked up to the mountain peak as they came to a halt beside the gate.

"Shit, is that another fire?" Tom shaded his eyes against the spring sunshine.

Levi reached behind him and pulled out the binoculars

he'd grabbed from his truck, training them on the second spiral of smoke heading skyward. It was separate to the first plume, which had grown in size and was now looking menacing. The second fire was farther up the mountain than the first, and more to the north.

"Yes, it is," Levi confirmed.

"Is it a spot fire, sparked from the first one?" Tom had dismounted from his quad and was opening the gate.

"I'm not sure. It looks too far away." Spot fires could sometimes start miles away from a major fire, but that was only if conditions were right, with strong winds and high heat in the middle of summer. Today was calm, barely a breath of wind, and the spring temperature while warm, still wasn't the blazing heat of mid-summer. The fuel load at this time of year would be low, with ground litter still damp from melting snow, and the deciduous trees only beginning to sprout green leaves. But a wildfire was still a wildfire, and they were damn dangerous, no matter if they were big or small. Tom glanced at him and they shared an unspoken question, which neither of them was game to say out loud. Was someone up there deliberately lighting fires? Given today's unseasonable heat, if someone was going to light a fire in spring, today had the perfect conditions for it.

Cat.

She was up there somewhere, possibly in danger. Did she even know about the fire? Or was she blissfully unaware that she had a growing inferno on her tail?

He needed to get up there and find Cat. Her name kept reverberating around in his brain, blocking all logical thought processes. He wanted to pump the throttle, point this quad up the hill and get up there as fast as was humanly possible. Depending where they were, she might not have seen the smoke. If they were headed upward, the trees and other ridgelines might hide it from view. Fire burned faster uphill.

It could catch them unaware.

Cat, where are you? His gaze scanned the mountains rising in front of them. His guts twisted in fear. Fear he might lose her.

"Let's go." Tom had the gate open; his four-wheeler was already through.

Levi tried to clear his head. He had things he needed to do. He needed to direct HQ to mobilize into immediate action. The forest service fire trucks might not make it all the way up there, but an air tanker could start dropping loads of water. At the moment, this fire wasn't even close to threatening homes or people in the small town of Stevensville, but they needed to be warned. Things could change in a heartbeat, fires could change direction, the wind could grow in strength.

"I've got to update HQ about this first."

"Right'o. Well, hurry up then." Tom drummed his fingers on the handlebars of his quad, his gaze fixed on the second smoke column. It was getting larger, even as they spoke.

Levi raised Thelma on his satellite phone and relayed his information quickly. She was fast and efficient, and he promised to call her back soon with more intel, while she got the fire department on route. He'd also requested an air tanker, which Thelma said she'd organize.

As he clicked the end button and put the radio back in his coat pocket, Tom gave a low whistle. "Holy shit, there's more smoke. That makes three." He turned toward Levi, his handsome face blanched white. "Someone is lighting fires up there."

CHAPTER FIFTEEN

"Keep going, Fiona, you're doing a great job." Cat kept her voice measured and reasonable. Her lungs were bursting as she sucked in deep gulps of air, and sweat was pouring off her, but she needed to keep pedaling. And she needed to stay calm. Only a hundred more feet or so to go. Smoke drifted past, but she ignored it. They had to reach the top of Romney Ridge. Her phone might get some reception up there. And it'd also give her a good vantage point, so she could get a better view of what was going on below them.

She snorted. A fire, that was what was going on. She already knew it. But how big, and in what direction was it traveling? They were the million-dollar questions.

She chanced a quick glance back at the young couple behind her. Charlie and Fiona. They were on their honeymoon and had come to Stargazer Ranch to spend a week in the mountains. Charlie was a keen outdoorsman, loved his hiking and camping. And Fiona was trying hard to please her new husband. They'd wanted to do a challenging mountain bike ride, and because everyone else was busy with other activities, Cat had offered to take them up Canyon Peak. She hadn't ridden a mountain bike since the last time she worked here, but she remembered the trails and winding pathways leading through the forest and had loved the exhilaration of racing down those steep, rocky slopes. The worst bit was the uphill climbs, like now. Especially in this warmer-than-usual weather. She'd already stripped off her coat and then her plaid shirt, and was down to her white T.

At least the wife was in good shape and had ridden mountain trails many times before. The couple had been happy about the bright, sunny day the weather gods had graced them with for this ride. Now, Cat was beginning to wonder if it was such a good thing after all. Fiona was around ten feet behind Cat, her face red and sweaty. But she had her head down, concentrating on navigating the tough terrain as she kept those pedals pumping. Charlie followed behind, his face grim. He was watching Fiona like a hawk; Cat could almost see him willing her to keep going.

Cat noticed the smoke when they'd stopped for a water break around a half hour earlier. At first, she hadn't been sure it was even smoke, thought it might've been low-lying mist still lifting from the mountain slope. But soon enough, they'd all caught a whiff, and Charlie had made a laughing comment, asking if it was their BBQ lunch he could smell.

Cat had remained tight-lipped, insisting that it wasn't wildfire season, and she could see it was only a small fire. Perhaps someone had left a campfire unattended. Keeping the conversation light, she told them it'd be an easy task, once they got to the top, to ride farther along the ridge, until they were out of the path of the fire, and then they could descend without a problem.

That was all true, until Cat had seen smoke from a second fire, coming from the direction she was intending on taking them. Almost as if someone had intentionally lit another blaze, cutting them off, forcing them to go in only one direction. Up.

Which was completely insane. No one was lighting fires.

Clayton was locked up in jail. But a tiny voice said she almost believed his tale; that he wasn't the arsonist. And if that were the case, then the real firebug was free to be out here doing whatever they wanted.

"I need to stop," Fiona called out.

Shit. Cat pedaled up to a flatter area and planted her feet on the ground. Plastering a smile of encouragement on her face, she turned to Fiona. The woman was around her own age, twenty-six or twenty-seven. She was pretty and blonde, taught elementary school for a living.

"You're doing great." Cat unclasped her backpack and got out a bottle of water. "Here you go, take a minute to get your breath back."

Charlie stopped his bike right behind Fiona's and cast Cat a significant look, meant only for her, telling her he realized exactly how much danger they were in. Then he too, plastered a smile on his face and said, "You're a star, my hunny-bunny. We're nearly there, look." He pointed to the ridge top, just visible through the branches.

"Will we be safe once we get up there?" Fiona puffed, her voice high-pitched and wobbly.

"Yes, we will. Cat will be able to call someone on her phone to come and get us. Then we can go back to the ranch and have a soak in that big tub in our honeymoon cabin." He grinned and patted his wife's bottom. Cat was glad he was trying to lighten the mood, because the last thing they needed was a hysterical woman on their hands. Cat nodded in agreement and glanced over the top of his wife's helmet, meeting his eyes and acknowledging his effort. Charlie was handsome, if you liked the muscle-bound type. He ran his own personal-training business. At least it meant he'd be an asset if they needed to hightail it out of there.

"Right, one last push and we're there," Cat said, focusing her gaze up the hill. She ignored the smoke growing thicker around them and tried not to cough. "Only a few more minutes, then we're safe." She crossed her fingers and hoped she was right.

For the next few minutes, Cat kept her head down and concentrated on pumping her legs. Up and down. Up and down. It was tough going, and although she liked to keep fit by running whenever she could, her legs were burning. It was getting so steep now, they might almost be better off ditching the bikes and walking the rest of the way. Except the bikes were going to be their ticket out of here, if she could work out which was the best way down. Her sore arm had almost recovered in the past few days, enough for her to keep the bandage off, now. She'd tied her coat and shirt to the pannier on the back of the bike, leaving her with only her white T-shirt on. Fiona had commented on the bruising and red marks on her arm, but Cat had waved off her concern, saying it was merely an accident.

Suddenly, her phone pinged in her jeans pocket. It was the sweetest sound Cat had heard in a long time. Then it pinged again. And again. Someone had desperately been trying to get hold of her. Perhaps she should've taken a set of two-way radios. Emily had taken a set out with her on the cattle drive today. But the radios only worked across shorter distances. A satellite phone was really what she needed. But Dean didn't enforce the need for his staff to carry one on a short trip like today, and so she hadn't bothered to ask for one from Gordon, before they left.

The top of Romney Ridge was flat and welcoming, and the vista of Bitterroot Valley could be seen below. But even from here, Cat couldn't quite see over the top of some of the taller fir trees to pinpoint exactly where the fire was. A granite outcrop of boulders ascended into the sky a few hundred feet away, and she made for that.

Checking to make sure the others were following, she

leaned her bike against a rock and said, "I'm going to climb up here. You two take a rest. There are granola bars and extra bottles of water in my backpack." She handed her bag over to Charlie and began to clamber upwards. She was desperate to check her phone, but wanted a better look at the fire first, so she could relay the whole situation back to Dean.

Glad her long legs made climbing that little bit easier, it still took her a few minutes to scramble all the way up. With a final heave, she made it to the top. She couldn't contain her gasp of shock and her stomach tightened at the sight before her.

The warm, spring sunshine, which had been so welcoming this morning, had turned an ominous orange, as smoke billowed all around, completely obscuring the blue sky. Now that she was above the tree line, she could see the two fires were indeed separate. The large one almost directly below them had taken serious hold. Dark smoke was filling the valley they'd just left behind, and orange flames flickered in the higher branches. It was almost as if someone had followed the exact same trail she and her guests had, only an hour or so behind them, lighting a fire directly on the path.

The second fire was around half a mile farther along, toward the edge of the escarpment. It was still below them, slightly higher and smaller than the first, the smoke a lighter grey, indicating it hadn't yet caught properly. But it was growing, and spreading, moving towards the first fire. One thing Cat knew about fire; it travelled faster uphill.

Because it was spring, everything remained damp, and this fire wasn't burning hot and fast as it would in summer. Which was a good thing. The pine needles on the ground would smolder before they caught, rather than blaze brightly, and it'd take a while for the undergrowth and bigger trees to properly catch alight. But the first fire seemed to be taking on a life of its own.

The Bitterroot Mountains were a series of rugged peaks, with numerous steep canyons cut into them by swift-running streams millions of years ago. They were some of the Northern Rockies' most rugged terrain. Beautiful, but also deadly, if you didn't know what you were doing.

She turned to her left, her gaze traveling west along the ridge they'd just ascended. A deep ravine split the ridgeline, so steep and rocky in places, it could almost be called a cliff. They couldn't get down that way. The only other route was to the right, down Canyon Creek Trail. But that was where the fires were headed. It was almost as if they were trapped. Being corralled into a smaller and smaller area. They could keep climbing, right to the top of Canyon Peak. But that'd be madness, because the fire would catch up with them eventually. Unless they could make it all the way up to the edge of the natural tree line, where the snow sat so long that nothing grew. Cat screwed up her eyes and looked upward. Nope, that wasn't an option. There was no way Fiona would make that distance.

Cat took her phone out of her jeans pocket and scrolled through the messages and texts. All of them from Dean. Until she got to the last one, which was from Levi.

Her chest ballooned at the sight of his name.

Why would Levi be calling her? What could he possibly want? She hadn't spoken to him since she'd stopped at his house three days ago. Her head had still been in turmoil over her discovery of her true feelings for Levi. And she wasn't sure how to approach them, or him, to find an answer. He'd never believe what was happening to her right now. She could hear his voice in her head, deep and melodious. He'd tell her this was no coincidence. Someone was causing mischief.

Cat dialed Dean's number.

He answered after only one ring, as if he'd been sitting by

the phone, waiting for her to call. "Cat, thank Christ." Dean exhaled on a gust of air. "Are you safe? Are the guests safe? How close is the fire?"

Cat followed Dean's lead, cutting straight to the chase. He knew they were in danger, so she didn't need to go into details. "We're on top of Romney Ridge. There's a big, rocky bluff. We're safe for the next few minutes. But we need a plan to get out of here."

"Great. Tom and Levi are on their way up to find you on four-wheelers. They've got a sat phone; I'll call them and give them your position. They left around twenty minutes ago."

What? Tom and Levi were coming? What was Levi doing here?

"How are they going to make it through the fires to get to us? They can't follow the same trail we took, it's consumed by flames. What about search and rescue? Don't they have a helicopter?"

"I don't know how Tom and Levi are going to get to you. But they can probably see what's going on as well as you can. Don't worry, they'll get up there somehow." Dean hesitated. "Search and rescue are busy up north with a climbing emergency."

Cat pursed her lips. In other words, Tom and Levi were their only option.

Shit. Something caught her attention. Were her eyes deceiving her? "Hang on a second, Dean." She took the phone away from her ear and squinted into the growing gloom. To where Canyon Creek Tail followed the ridge along the side of the mountain. It was her one escape plan. If they could ride fast enough along the top, they might outrun the flames to get past them, then descend the mountain that way. It'd mean they'd end up a long way from the ranch, but at least they'd be on the valley floor and away from the creeping flames.

But now…there was smoke coming from where the trail cut along the ridgeline, around a mile away.

She brought the phone slowly up to her mouth again. "Things just got a whole lot worse," she said slowly. "There's another fire. This one's on the trail. Along the direct line of our only possible escape. Someone is out here, Dean. And they're trying to burn us alive."

CHAPTER SIXTEEN

Levi listened to Tom's one-sided conversation as he talked with Dean on the sat phone. He drummed his fingers on the handlebars, gaze fixed on the mountain towering above them. She was up there, somewhere. Hopefully beyond the fire now barring their way. His hands twitched with the need to push the start button on the four-wheeler and careen up the slope, ignoring the smoke and flames a few hundred feet above them.

It'd only taken around ten minutes to get here once they got through the gate at the fence line, following the same trail Cat and her guests had taken. Cat had probably taken half an hour or so to cover the same distance on their mountain bikes. Whoever had lit the fires must be either on horseback, motorcycle, or four-wheeler. Because there was no way they were moving around this terrain so quickly otherwise.

A large, blackened area sat between them and the slow-moving fire. The smoke wasn't too bad, the air relatively clear, a slight breeze blowing the fumes up the mountain. This gave them an excellent view of the way the wildfire was spreading. It was much too big to try putting it out. The fire didn't seem to be extending downhill at all, as if the steep slope was enough to defeat it. He and Tom had beaten out a row of smoldering flames nearby, stopping it from spreading to a patch of bushes. The flames marched a long way in either direction, parallel to the line of the slope. Which was weird. The only explanation Levi could come up with was that someone had walked in a straight line, dropping matches, or using a drip torch, like the local forest fire services when they carried out controlled burns to reduce fuel loads before the summer wildfire season. The more he looked at it, the more he was sure that's what had happened. Some bastard had intentionally lit this fire and made sure the fire spread as far as possible to catch anyone in its path.

Levi had already called in to HQ, relaying everything he could see to Thelma. Two forest fire trucks were already on their way up a service road through the state forest toward them. Another two teams were checking their maps for fire trails farther up on Canyon Peak; anticipating further instructions from Levi as to the direction and speed of the fire. He was still waiting to hear about the air tanker.

"Right'o, boss, I've got all that. Let me talk to Levi and see if we can work something out. I'll call you back in a minute." Tom moved the phone away from his ear and turned to study Levi, whose heart sank at the look in Tom's eyes.

"The good news is, Dean's made contact with Cat. She and the couple are up on Romney Ridge near Loneman's Bluff. You know that tall outcrop of boulders?"

Levi nodded his head. Good. That was great news. They should be safe up there. At least for a while. "And the bad news?" he asked, tapping the tip of his boot on the foot pegs.

"That third plume of smoke we saw. It is another fire, and it looks like it started directly on Canyon Creek Trail."

Shit. That was the only safe way out of there for Cat and the others. He and Tom had been figuring out the best way to get to the top of the ridge, counting on Cat doing the same, hoping to find her up there. And Cat had done what they expected. Except now, every second they sat here talking, the fire was cutting them off. He racked his brain to come up with a solution. If they could get the air tanker in the air, it might be able to drop a load or two on the trail, clear a path for Cat and her guests. Give them a bit more breathing space. An air tanker wouldn't be able to douse the whole fire, it was too big, but it could definitely make a dent in its momentum.

Before Levi could open his mouth to convey his idea, his phone rang.

It was Thelma, and Levi's heart sank as he listened. He thanked her and hung up.

"That didn't sound like good news, judging by the look on your face." Tom frowned at him.

"Nope. There are two air tankers in Montana and both of them are unavailable. One was damaged in that big storm we had the other night, and the other has been called away to fight another fire over on the far edge of the state."

"Shit." Tom didn't need to say any more, that one word conveyed it all.

"We'll just have to get up there on our own, then," Levi said, thinking fast. "I reckon, if we can find a way through the flames, we can easily outrun the fire on the quads." Levi eyed the flames above, looking for a spot where they weren't as dense, an unburned patch he could weave his way through. "If we head farther east, there could still be a gap between these two fires. They might not have joined up yet." With the mountain rescue helicopter tied up at Kootenai Canyon for the next few hours, at least, he and Tom were Cat's only hope.

Tom raised a hand, palm outward. "Slow down. I'm just as desperate as you are to bring them down alive. But we need to be smart about this."

Levi shook his head. Tom's feelings didn't even begin to compare to what he was experiencing right now. Yes, Tom might be desperate to get the honeymoon couple back. It might ruin Stargazer Ranch's reputation forever, if someone were to die in a wildfire while staying here. But that didn't come close to how frantic Levi was to find Cat.

Tom wasn't in love with one of the people trapped up on the mountain.

It took Levi a few seconds to process that thought.

Love.

He was in love with Cat.

Always had been. Always would be.

He forced that thought from his mind. No time for that, now.

"Let's say we do manage to get up to the top of the ridge." Tom said. "How do we get back down, once we have them?"

That was a more interesting question, and Levi had to agree it was one he didn't have an answer for. But he'd work something out. They had to. Otherwise, Cat might die.

"What about taking the ridgeline to the west? Where the ravine cuts through it." Levi asked, thinking aloud. "I've seen the topographical map and Dean told me about the terrain. I've never been up there. Is the ravine really that bad? Could we perhaps climb down that way? Even if we couldn't get the bikes down?"

"Not without ropes," Tom said, shaking his head. "I haven't personally climbed up there, we don't have the expertise on the ranch to do that. But Jason—he runs the Extreme Mountain Sports team up in Missoula—has taken a few of our keen guests up there." Tom passed the sat phone back and forth between his hands, glancing up at the deep ravine, which was more of a scar running right through the middle of the ridge, almost to the top of Canyon Peak. "He won't take beginners up there. Says it's pretty rough, and there's a couple of overhangs you can only manage with ropes."

"Okay, so that way is definitely out." Levi caught himself

stroking his beard as he thought out loud. It was becoming a habit.

"What about the other side of Romney Ridge? Doesn't it dip down again on the other side, before the slope starts to climb up to the peak? I have a vague memory of a shallow valley running parallel to the ridge for quite a way."

Tom's face lit up. "I think you're right. Could we follow that valley until we get past the fire zone, then head down?"

"Fire doesn't run nearly as quick downhill as it does up," Levi replied. "So even the fire that's burning along the top of the ridge shouldn't spread too fast into that dale." His mind was trying to do the calculations, but in the end, he had to give up. There was no way they could know how far or fast the third fire was spreading until they got there. It could already be eating its way into their only escape route, for all they knew.

Tom had his gaze fixed on the mountain above, as if weighing up all his options. But Levi was over waiting. The one thing he knew for certain, Cat was up there, in the direct path of the fire, and he needed to get there to help her.

"I'm going," Levi stated flatly. HQ had told him to wait for the fire engines to arrive, so he could fill them in, but that wasn't going to happen. They'd sort out the priorities soon enough once they got here. "I don't care whether you come or not. I'll aim for that gap over there." He pointed to a clearing around three hundred feet up the slope and to their left, where green grass could still be seen amongst the smoldering leaf litter. It formed a natural fire break in the line of flames advancing up the hill. Smoke and ash prevented him from seeing farther into the forest, so he couldn't be sure there wasn't a raging inferno waiting for him on the other side, but he was prepared to take the chance.

"Settle down." Tom waved a hand at him. "Like I said before, I'm as keen to rescue them as you are. I just don't want to get barbecued in the process." Tom readjusted his quad helmet, fiddling with the strap as he spoke. "And you need me to come with you. How else were you figuring on getting three extra people to safety on one quad?"

"I would've found a way," Levi said, but in truth he hadn't been sure, himself. The Stargazer quads had been specifically made to carry two people. Which meant they were larger and heavier than a single-person machine, but much more versatile. They also had a metal rack behind the second seat, designed to strap on a bag or carry a piece of equipment. But someone could also sit on it, in an emergency.

"I'll let Dean know our plan of action. I can already tell you, he's not going to like it." Tom lowered his eyebrows in a frown. "But I'll make him see there's no other alternative."

Levi waited, fingers twitching, and muscles tensed, while Tom phoned his boss. His replies were short and terse, and a few times Levi could hear Dean's raised voice on the other end of the line. But eventually Tom rang off, his brow set in a determined line.

He nodded and Tom winked back. Levi was eternally grateful that the man was courageous and steadfast enough to risk this crazy plan with him. Levi also readjusted his helmet, making sure it wouldn't to come off. This was going to be one hell of a ride. He pulled up the bandana he had purposefully wrapped around his neck to cover his mouth and nose and made sure his coat was zipped all the way up. He already had gloves on. The heat of the day was already making him sweat with all these extra layers. It wasn't ideal firefighting equipment, but he hoped it'd be enough protection to get him through to the other side. Tom did the same.

"Ready?"

"As I'll ever be," Tom replied.

Levi took off, revving the engine hard, gaining speed as

they raced up the mountain. The quad handled the terrain well, running over the small rocks and gravel with ease. Levi dodged a couple of larger, rocky outcrops and clumps of bushes. The ground in front of them was already burnt and some of it still smoked and fumed.

The green grass of the small clearing was a beacon, calling him on. The quad tires ran over the smoking leaf litter and he hoped the black rubber was tough enough to withstand the added damage from the heat as well as the sharp surface of the forest floor.

They were going to make it; he could see a pathway through the worst of the fire, between the trees on the other side of the opening. They might have to dodge around a few burning tree trunks, but as long as they didn't run into a huge pile of hot coals, they could get through this.

He was halfway through the grassy clearing when he spotted the deep gulley blocking their path on the other side. He slammed on the brakes and Tom nearly collided into the back of him. If they tried to ride through that, the quads would get stuck, for sure.

"We'll have to go around it," Tom yelled above the sound of the crackling fire. Levi hadn't noticed while he was riding, but wildfires had a noise all of their own. It was a little like the roar of a small airplane high above. And the whoosh of air as the flames sucked in all the available oxygen. Add to that the crackle and hiss of pine bark catching fire, and it was more than a little eerie. The smoke wasn't too heavy here, but it would be farther up, when they got upwind of the fire.

Looking upslope, Levi identified where the ditch began, in a natural hollow in the ground. Above it, the ground was flat and safe. Problem was, the hollow was right beneath a large stand of fir trees, whose higher branches were blazing brightly. They were well and truly alight and looked to have been burning for a while. He hunkered down low, ducking his head almost to the level of the handlebars, and took a deep breath.

Then he was off. Keeping the quad in low gear, so he had more control, he zoomed along the edge of the ditch. Tom was close on his tail; he could hear the buzz of his motor behind him. Gauging the flames as he got closer, he noted the tops of the trees were flaming like bright signal fires as the fire crawled up the combustible bark. This was going to be dodgy as hell. And now it wasn't only the tires he was worried about. If one of those flying embers or a hot coal got kicked up into the engine or the exhaust system, the quad could break down halfway through the inferno. Both he and Tom were also highly vulnerable to all the hot ash and sparks flying through the air. They were crazy to be attempting this. He weaved through the tree trunks, keeping as close to the dip in the ground as he could, where the trees were thinnest.

Cat. He needed to help Cat. He kept an image of her fixed firmly in his mind as he rode forward. This was for her. To save her.

Then they were underneath the flaming trees. It was hard to tell the earth from the sky; everything was a swirling mass of smoke and heat. A burning branch fell from high up. He heard it crashing through the other branches toward the ground. At the last moment, he zigged left on instinct, and felt a rush of sparks and debris brush past his right side. He caught the smell of singed hair as the flames licked over his helmet and let out a yell of fear and adrenaline. But he had no choice; he had to keep going, and hope Tom was doing the same.

CHAPTER SEVENTEEN

The smoke was getting thicker. Cat had made makeshift rags for the other two to tie around their mouths and noses from a dishcloth Stella had packed in with their lunch. She was using her trusty, red bandana for herself. Fiona coughed loudly. Cat stopped and took out a bottle of water. It was their last; they needed to conserve it.

"Here, wet the fabric again," she said, passing the bottle back "It helps keep out the smoke. But please don't use all the water," she cautioned.

"The fire's getting closer." Fiona's eyes were wide and dark, the only things visible above the rag covering her face.

"I know." Cat glanced back the way they'd come. The wildfire was indeed creeping over the crest of the ridge behind them, engulfing the pile of boulders she'd been standing on only fifteen minutes ago. Loneman's Bluff, Dean had called it.

"I mean the one in front of us." Fiona pointed an unsteady finger.

Cat was well aware of that one. The second fire had now grown and enlarged and would soon crest the top of the ridgeline. Effectively cutting them off from the only path out of here. Even if they didn't take into account the third fire lit on the trail directly downhill of them.

Dean had contacted her and told her Levi and Tom were on their way up, and all she had to do was sit tight till they got there. Which would've been fine, if the fire hadn't picked up pace and climbed quickly toward them. When Cat had asked Dean about search and rescue; about requesting a helicopter extraction, he'd told her the depressing news. They were tied up with another retrieval. As Cat looked at the encroaching flames, she doubted a helicopter would've been able to get close to them, anyway. It would've been too dangerous. Cat had no choice but to move away from Loneman's Bluff, following the path along the top of the ridge. She was intent on getting this young couple out of here. They'd have a wild story to tell their grandkids about their honeymoon that went up in flames. But Cat was determined they would live to *have* grandkids. She knew what she was doing. She hoped.

Dean had also mentioned Levi's plan for escape was to drop down into the shallow dale on the mountain side of Romney Ridge and use that as an escape route. The fire would burn much slower on the downward slope, giving them enough time to outrun it. The only problem was, it'd slow them down considerably on their bicycles if they had to pick their way through the rough mountainside. And if that didn't work, then they'd have to find a cave or somewhere else to shelter, and hopefully ride out the wildfire that way.

Her main aim right now was to keep Fiona calm. Charlie was holding it together with grim determination, but it was for his wife's benefit, as much as his own.

"Yep, I see it," Cat said, offering the water to Charlie to wet down his face mask. Even if she hadn't been able to see the flames with her own eyes, Cat could feel the increasing heat, rising up the mountain along the fire front. The urge to unzip her coat and fling it off was strong, sweat was trickling down her back and her face was flushed with heat. But that was her best protection against the flames.

"Do your coat back up," she snapped, as she noticed Fiona had undone the buttons on her coat.

"But I'm so hot," Fiona grumbled, then coughed loudly.

"It's for your own safety, hunny-bunny." Charlie moved his bicycle over and helped Fiona do her buttons back up.

"Thanks," Cat replied, reining in her impatience. With one final glance at the oncoming fire, she made a decision. "We're going to head down this incline. It looks as good a place as any." Cat kept her voice light.

"But that's going in the wrong direction." Fiona's voice gained a note of hysteria. "We need to go back to the ranch, not farther up the mountain."

Cat bit her tongue, but before she could come up with a suitably calm reply, Charlie said, "Look, Fi, we need to trust Cat. If she says she knows a way out of here, then we have to follow her." He didn't say it, but he glanced toward the oncoming fire, then back at the fire behind them. They were being hemmed in. Soon, there'd be no way out.

Cat cast him a grateful glance and pointed her bicycle down the slope. It was steeper than the one they'd climbed, but there were fewer trees and less vegetation, something to do with the angle of the north face and how much sun it got, or some such mumbo jumbo. Levi would be able to explain it, if he were here. Levi. She'd intentionally kept her mind away from any thought of him.

But now that she knew he was making his way up the mountain to come for her, he grew larger in her thoughts. She couldn't explain the gratitude and feeling of safety that idea brought with it. Levi was coming for her. It was stupid and irrational, but she couldn't help feeling everything would be fine, if only she could see his face once more. That crooked smile he kept just for her. The way she felt like she was drowning whenever she looked too long into his brown eyes. Even though Cat had fought against it tooth and nail, Levi had planted a hook deep in her chest, and, like a fish caught on a line, she would never get free. She could admit he'd captivated her the very first time she'd set eyes on him. He owned a piece of her soul. And no matter how far or fast she ran, he'd always live inside her. Even after six months spent trying to rid herself of his essence, it'd only grown stronger, calling her back to Bitterroot Valley.

Her bike bumped over a large rock and she nearly fell. Shit. She needed to focus, get her mind away from Levi. The bottom of the shallow valley lay about a quarter mile below them, but even from here, Cat could see it'd be hard to plot a course down through the roughly strewn boulders and rocky outcrops. The last thing they needed was for someone to fall and break a leg. Then they'd be completely at the mercy of the fire. She corralled all thoughts of Levi into a box in her mind and slammed the lid shut. There'd be time to dwell on this attraction; this bond between them later. She had to get them all safely out of here, first.

As Cat negotiated her way around a fallen log and between two large boulders, she wondered for the hundredth time who could be doing this? Who was out here, intentionally lighting fires? Because there was no doubt in her mind, she was the target of a firebug. But why? Clayton was still in jail. Could he possibly have an accomplice? Was he directing this from behind bars? It seemed highly unlikely. Which meant Clayton's claims of innocence might well be true, after all.

Dean had been informed by Deputy Wilder just this morning that one of the three main people of interest he'd named in the interview the other day, was no longer a suspect. Mathew Davis, the previous owner of Stargazer Ranch had died of a heart attack nearly a year ago. And the sheriff had already cleared Mike Spencer, so she could cross him off the list. But what about the other two? Dean's ex-girlfriend and the guy who'd worked for him. They must be some kind of twisted people if they could do this to him…to her. The police needed to start digging deeper and figure out who was doing this. Before it was too late.

A glance back showed the ridgeline now completely engulfed in flames. She'd made the right decision to descend when she did. But now they only had a few hundred feet between them and the encroaching fire front.

They'd nearly made it to the floor of the valley, when her phone rang. She rounded a large pine tree and found a good place to stop, checking Fiona and Charlie were safely on her tail. Thankful her phone still had reception, she pulled it out and checked caller ID.

Levi. Her heart did a little happy dance in her chest.

"Hello, Levi," she said.

"Cat, thank God you're still okay." Levi sounded out of breath. Cat couldn't suppress the shudder of joy that twisted through her belly at the sound of his voice. "We made it to the top of the ridge. Where are you?"

"On our way into the shallow valley on the other side," Cat replied. "Nearly at the bottom. We had to leave Canyon Creek Trail; the second fire cut us off." It was a little ironic—the arsonist hadn't needed to light the third fire, because in the end the second blaze had already done its job and stopped their escape.

"Good. That's good, Cat." She could hear the relief in his voice and imagined the slight smile that news might bring to his lips. "Can you ride east, along the bottom of the valley? We had to detour around the second and third fires. We'll ride up the valley to meet you. There's a small lake about a half a mile from where you are. It's called Lomo Lake. If we lose phone reception, we'll meet you there."

"Got it. Levi…" Cat hesitated.

"What? What is it, Cat?"

"Thank you. Thank you for coming." She hoped he could hear everything else she couldn't say in those few words.

"There's nowhere I'd rather be, than rescuing your ass from yet another fire," he joked. But she caught the serious note at the back of his humor. He got it. He got how much she appreciated him. How much she needed him.

"See you in a little while," she said, getting her business persona back on and ending the call.

"They're almost here," Cat called over her shoulder to Fiona and Charlie, giving them a thumbs-up. "They're going to meet us at a lake. Not too far now."

"That's great," Charlie called back. Fiona gave a little whimper of what Cat hoped was gratitude. But one look at her face told her Fiona was close to breaking point. She didn't have a lot more in her. Thank God, Levi and Tom were close. Cat hated to think what might've happened if, for some reason, they hadn't decided to brave the fire and mount a rescue. With the helicopter unavailable, Fiona may not have made it back down the mountain, otherwise.

Cat had a sudden awful thought. Perhaps the arsonist hadn't been so dumb lighting that third fire, after all. Because if the second fire was already climbing over Romney Ridge, then the third fire, lit on the highest point, might already be much farther down into this small valley.

Cat stood up on her pedals as she let the bike coast down the last incline, trying to see east, along the length of the depression. All that was visible was more smoke. It got thicker farther down, obscuring everything in its path, so Cat had no idea what was waiting for them. She'd have to trust Levi and follow his instructions, because from here, it looked like they were heading into the pits of hell, not away from them.

CHAPTER EIGHTEEN

"I can see them." Tom was slightly in front of Levi, standing up on his four-wheeler as they wove their way slowly through the thick smoke. Levi's heart leapt at Tom's words. "They're over on the other side of the lake. Cat is waving at us."

Levi surged forward on his quad and squinted into the gloom. Smoke wafted in great billows down the valley, but as the air cleared slightly, Levi could make out three figures, all waving madly, standing on the northern-most point of the small lake—if it could be called that; it was more of a large pond, only about a hundred feet or so wide—their bicycles scattered on the rocky ground a few feet away. Canyon Creek ran right through this valley and formed a series of small lakes in its path. In summer, most of these lakes would be almost dry, but now, with all the snow melt, they were full to the brim.

"We need to hurry." That might be the understatement of the year. It'd taken them longer than they anticipated to wind their way up the narrow ravine, as it'd been rocky and almost impassable in places. It'd be tricky to get back down, especially with extra passengers onboard.

Flames licked at a stand of oak trees on the other side of

the lake. The fire was already in the long grass surrounding the edge of the water. At least the grass was green and lush, not tinder-dry, like it would've been in the middle of summer.

Levi pushed his thumb a little harder on the throttle, eager to get around the lake to Cat. The quad stuttered for a second, but then leapt ahead. It was the third time in the past few minutes his quad had acted strangely. But he had no time to stop and check it now. It could be a number of things, perhaps the air intake had become clogged with ash and dust. At least all four tires seemed to be holding up. The best he could do was to keep his fingers crossed that the vehicle got them back down the hill in one piece.

The three shadowy figures morphed out of the smoke, and Levi focused on Cat's tall, lithe frame. She had on her new, bulky Stargazer coat, a bicycle helmet and a bandana covering her face. But he knew it was her. His body would recognize her anywhere.

Stopping his quad right in front of Cat, he switched it off and practically leapt over the handlebars. Then he had her in his arms, sweeping her off her feet, so he could hold her body close. To make sure she was real. That she was alive and in one piece.

"Levi," she said, with a surprised squeak.

"I don't care," he growled, when she cast a quick glance at the others, now standing watching the spectacle. "I need to hold you. To make sure you're all right."

She stared back at him, her blue eyes bright and clear. He did the only thing possible. Yanked down her bandana and kissed her. Fierce and quick. Enough for her to know how he felt. Then he let her go and stepped away as he cast an appraising gaze over the two guests. They looked young and fit, but while the man seemed to be in control, the woman had an overwrought look in her eyes. All three of them were smeared with soot and ash, like they had just come through the pits of hell. They'd made it this far, but they still had to get down off this flaming mountainside.

"Can you fit both of them on the back of your quad?" he demanded of Tom. It was a gamble, putting three people on one quad, but they had no other choice. He and Tom had discussed it on the way up. Tom was riding a newer, slightly more powerful quad. So, he'd take the married couple, the woman on the seat behind him and the man on the wire rack at the back, holding onto the rear bar. Levi would take Cat on the back of his quad.

"Yes." Tom had come to the same conclusion as Levi, that the muscle-bound husband should be able to hold on at the back on the wild ride down the hill.

"Good, Cat, you're with me." He handed her the spare helmet hanging from the back, which she swapped out for her mountain bike helmet.

Tom jumped on his quad and started it up, motioning for the woman to get on behind him. Which she did, after first sending a questioning gaze toward her husband. He nodded and settled himself onto the rack at the back. It wouldn't be comfortable, and he might have a bruised backside when he got to the ranch, but it'd work. Tom only had one spare helmet, which the man helped his wife put on.

Levi leaped onto his quad and turned the ignition to on. Then he pushed the throttle with his thumb, expecting to hear the motor come to life.

There was silence.

He tried again.

Nothing.

The quad was dead.

Levi checked the oncoming fire. A huddle of bushes halfway around the lake burst into flames.

He tried again to start it. And again.

"Why aren't we moving?" Fiona squealed.

Tom's gaze narrowed as he stared at Levi's quad. Levi shook his head and motioned for Cat to dismount.

If Tom didn't leave now, it'd be too late for him and the young couple to get out.

"You go," he yelled. "If I can get it started, I'll follow you. If not, we'll take shelter in the lake." Levi clambered off the quad and stood next to Cat, who hadn't said a word.

"We're not going without you." But even as Tom said the words, both men knew they weren't true. Tom had a responsibility to make sure the two guests survived.

"You need to go," Levi repeated. His riveted his gaze on Tom. The big man was courageous, and Levi had no doubt he'd stay until the bitter end. But he had a job to do. Big Tom closed his eyes for a second, as if internally debating his answer. When he opened them, Levi could see his reply written in the depths. He'd do the right thing, even though it was nearly killing him to leave Cat and Levi.

"You go, Tom," Cat said into the ominous silence. "We'll be okay. See you back at the ranch." This last comment was for Fiona and Charlie, reassuring them, so they wouldn't panic. She was doing her job, too. Staying strong for the guests. But that was Cat all over, she was a strong woman. They'd get through this.

"Stay in touch, if you can." Tom's normally jovial face was pale and full of angst. Slowly, he turned to the front of his quad and they moved away, Charlie glancing back at them.

Levi scrambled to take off his helmet, so he could inspect the quad. He got down on his knees. It was hard to see anything up under the wheel hub with his eyes stinging with smoke, but even from here he noticed something dripping from a piece of black tubing. He dipped a finger in the stuff and sniffed. Oil. The quad was leaking oil. Not good. On closer inspection he could see some of the tubes and wiring were smoldering. Sparks or coals had become lodged and had burned through the rubber. This quad was going nowhere.

"What's the verdict?" Cat peered over his shoulder.

"Dead as a doornail. I'm surprised it even got me this far."

She gave him an unreadable glance, then began fumbling with the strap under her chin. When she couldn't undo it, she gave an impatient stamp of her foot.

"Here, let me." Levi gently brushed her hands out of the way and undid the buckle. He lifted the helmet and tossed it in the long grass, setting her blonde hair free. His fingers lingered on her skin. She was warm and alive. And he needed her to stay that way.

"Why don't you let the mechanic take a look?" She practically pushed him out of the way and knelt down next to the quad. At least her snarky side was still alive and well. She poked around and muttered under her breath for a few moments, then stood up next to him.

"Dead as a doornail?" He couldn't help it, he had to ask. Because he already knew that not even the best mechanic in the world could fix a melted oil line. Not without the correct parts and a fair bit of time. Both of which they didn't have.

She ignored him, asking instead, "What are we going to do? The fire's nearly here." Her gaze flicked over his shoulder. "We've still got the mountain bikes; we could try them."

Levi looked at the bikes and then at the flames, which seemed to have picked up speed. The stand of oaks on the other side of the lake was completely engulfed now, dark smoke spiraling skywards. The rest of the surrounding pine forest on that side of the valley was also blazing brightly. As he assessed their situation, one of the pine trees exploded, sending sparks and shards of wood flying in all directions, and they both ducked.

"I don't think we'd make it," Levi shouted. They had one

last option. He grabbed her hand and brought it up to his lips. "But we're not going to give up." He turned her to face the small lake. "If we can shelter long enough, the fire will pass us by."

Levi removed his phone from his coat pocket. He held Cat's hand and they waded into the murky water together. It was freezing, and Cat sucked in a sudden gasp. This lake would've had a layer of thick ice on it less than a month ago, and the water was only just above freezing.

"Great choice you've given me. Either freeze to death in a mountain lake or get barbecued by a wildfire. Not sure I like either of those options, Mr. Wilson."

Cat turned to him. Her face was lined with soot and worry, but her eyes flashed crystalline blue in the dim light. She lifted her studded eyebrow and gave him that look. That one of feisty determination. The one she'd given him on that very first day, when he'd pulled her out of the burning cabin and she'd haughtily told him she did not need rescuing, thank you very much. In that second, he'd been captivated by her. Unable to look away. If he admitted it, that was when he'd fallen for Catriona Lawson.

After she left him, ran away on her motorcycle because she couldn't handle the commitment of a relationship, he'd thought of it as her greatest flaw. Her stubborn independence stopped her from truly loving someone. From truly letting them into her heart. But now he saw perhaps it was also her greatest asset. If she were any less of a woman, any less gutsy and undaunted, she might not have made it this far. Might not make it through the next few hours. And he needed her to make it.

"I'm not sure I like them, either," he agreed. "Give me your phone. I'll try and keep it dry," he added. She handed him her cell and they walked forward.

At least the small lake wasn't deep, and they managed to

wade almost to the middle, where the water lapped halfway up his belly. The icy water took his breath away. Even though the air around them was hot, and getting hotter by the second, the shock of the cold was harsh. He wasn't sure how long they could stay here before their legs went numb and stopped holding them up. There was still the high chance they'd succumb to smoke inhalation. If the oxygen levels dropped, one or both of them could pass out. And if they were in the water when that happened, well... The idea didn't bear thinking about.

"Take your coat off." He did the same, and showed her how to hold it over her head, like a small tent. "This'll keep the smoke and ash out." They stood huddled together beneath their little makeshift shelter, their foreheads touching. It was almost peaceful in here, the raging fire now muffled by the thick coats. The only sound was that of their shuddering breaths, as they fought against the cold and terror.

Levi peeked out through a gap in the fabric. The fire had almost fully encircled the lake, now. There was no going back; they were trapped, and at the mercy of the flames. It was like they were in the middle of a raging bonfire. The fire created its own micro weather system, and gusts of wind buffeted them from all around. The smoke wasn't bad inside their tent, so he pulled down his bandana. Cat did the same. He kept both of their phones held up out of the water. Hope lingered, that if they got out of this alive, they might be able to call Tom and arrange a rescue.

Cat's teeth began to chatter, the noise loud inside their confined space. "I'm just cold," she said defensively, and Levi almost smiled. Trust Cat to not want him to think her chattering teeth were from fear.

"I know, so am I." He tilted her chin up, so he could look straight in her eyes. "But, Cat, I'm also terrified. I don't want to die out here. I don't want you to die out here." He let her see the truth of his words as he stared into her face. He was truly petrified. But he wouldn't want to be anywhere else, either. If Cat had to endure this, then he was glad he was here to endure it with her. Together, they'd make it through.

"It's okay to be scared," she blurted, and he knew she hadn't thought about her words, that she was merely trying to placate him. It was a rote reply, one she didn't think applied to her. This was probably the worst place and the worst time to be having this conversation. But Levi wanted Cat to know how he truly felt. It was now or never.

"I know it's okay to be scared. But do you know that, Cat?" he asked gently. "Do you know it's okay to be vulnerable every once in a while? It won't make me think any less of you."

Cat's teeth stopped chattering for a second as she regarded him.

"You know I'm in love with you, Cat. That I don't ever want to lose you again."

There it was. He'd laid his cards on the table. His heart thudded louder in his chest than it had on the whole way up here, as he waited for her answer.

CHAPTER NINETEEN

Fire raged around them. Yet Cat was riveted to Levi's words, more petrified of what he'd said than of the fire waiting to consume them along the perimeter of the lake.

She opened her mouth and shut it again. Her thoughts tumbled like boulders down a mountain, out of control and hurtling toward an unknown fate.

Levi spoke into the silence of their makeshift cocoon. "I'm not afraid of you, Cat. I can see now, most men are intimidated by you. You're a strong woman; some might even call you reckless. And that's the way you want it. It's your protection, your armor against the world."

His words sank deep into her heart. But instead of feeling like a knife blade had cut her open, they were a balm to soothe her soul. A part of Cat knew he was speaking the truth. Right from an early age, Cat was convinced she was emotionally stunted. You could blame her father for his rough, careless handling of his only daughter, or her mother dying when she was so young, or all the other sad and sorry tales that made up her life. But the truth was, she was missing a part of her heart. Or rather, had shut that piece of her heart away for safekeeping. And the way she covered it up was to be so single-minded and self-sufficient that she showed the world she didn't need anyone else. But Levi saw through all that. Saw through to the vulnerable woman she was underneath. He wasn't threatened by her need to seem invincible. She'd always known Levi understood her on some deeper level. And perhaps that was what scared her the most.

Levi continued, and her mind scrambled to keep up. "But I also know what I want in a woman. I want her to be committed to me. One-hundred-percent. Or not at all. I don't want to love someone who won't love me back. Not *can't* love me back. But *won't*. Do you get that, Cat?"

The air was tense in the dim closeness of the coat tent and she kept her chin lowered, staring at the water lapping around her middle. She couldn't look at him. But she knew Levi's beautiful, brown eyes would be fixed on her. He wanted a commitment from her. That she would stay this time. Stay and make it work. But she was so terrified she would fail him. Again. She wasn't robust enough emotionally to deal with the intensity he was bound to demand from her.

Or was she?

Levi was her complete opposite. He was in touch with his feelings, emotionally strong. But maybe that meant he could cope with her emotional weaknesses. People talked about Yin and Yang, about opposites making each other stronger, complementing each other, connecting them on some genuine level.

Her bottom lip trembled. What the hell? Was she turning into some little namby-pamby crybaby, now? Or were her teeth chattering again?

She suddenly became aware that her lower half was so cold it was like hundreds of tiny knives shooting up her legs. She moved, trying to ease the torture in her thighs and calves.

Levi noticed her grimace and brought her chin up with one hand so he could see her face. "I'm sorry, Cat. I know this is not the best time or place to be bringing this up. All I really want you to know is, I love you. Heart and soul. The rest is up to you."

How did she answer that kind of declaration? Her teeth began to chatter again, and this time her whole body shook with the cold. Could she love him the way he deserved to be loved?

His arm came around her shoulders. "We need to get out of here. It won't do us any good if we escape from the fire, only to die of hypothermia." He lifted the edge of his coat and they both peered out through the gap.

The scene before them wasn't of complete devastation, as Cat had been expecting. The stand of oak trees was still blazing at the other end of the lake, but it'd soon burn itself out. One of the trees had already fallen over and lay smoking on the blackened ground. But there were still tufts of green grass around the edge of the lake, the lush dampness having defeated even the hungriest of flames. The main fire front had passed them by, and flames could be seen marching toward the farthest slope, picking up speed as they went. The landscape it left behind was a black ruin, like something out of a dystopian apocalypse movie. Most of the pine trees still smoked like chimneys, and a large clump of wild blackberry burned nearby.

"I think it's safe," Levi murmured.

Cat nodded in agreement. The heat of a passing wildfire would almost be welcome, after this eternal cold that was eating into her bones.

Levi slowly lifted his coat from around his head and held it above the water, making sure it stayed dry. She followed his lead as they waded toward shore. Her wet jeans clung to her thighs as water sluiced off them. She was shaking almost uncontrollably. Both of their coats had scorch marks on them, where blazing embers had clearly landed during the height of the fire.

"Watch out, the ground will still be hot in places. If you're not careful, it'll melt right through your boots." Levi took her hand to help her out of the water, and they stood on the edge of the shoreline, surveying the destruction around them.

The mountain bikes were a pile of twisted metal, and Levi's four-wheeler was a lump of melted plastic and smoldering rubber.

He took Cat's coat from her hands and wrapped it around her, rubbing her arms as he tried to warm her up. She looked up into his face. His lips were blue, and his teeth were chattering, as well. But he was taking the time to make sure she was okay first. Her gaze traced his forehead, following the line of his straight nose, and then roamed over his high cheekbones, bronze skin, and full lips. His long hair was a straggly mess, strands hanging down each side of his face, catching in his beard.

When the fire had been right on her tail as she'd been leading Fiona and Charlie up the mountain, the only thing that'd kept her going was the thought of Levi. She'd held his face foremost in her mind and knew if she could make it to the top of the ridge, he'd come for her.

"Thank you." She reached up to touch his cheek. It was nice to have someone take care of her. And he wanted to take care of her, if she'd only let him. Why was she trying to fight this thing? She was beginning to lose all her reasons, all her justifications for living a separate life, free of any complications. Because Levi wasn't a complication, he was a gift. If only she'd let her frozen heart open enough to let him in.

"You're welcome." He didn't turn away, as if he could tell she had more to say. His dark gaze bored into hers, waiting.

She let her hand fall to his shoulder, then her fingers wrapped around the nape of his neck. A flash of hope flared in his earth-colored eyes. She gravitated up, drawn to his lips, and kissed him. Long and deep. Something inside her melted at the touch of his lips. Her shaking stopped as she concentrated on him, and only him.

"I want to be your one-hundred-percent woman," she whispered against his neck.

She knew he needed to hear it; knew she needed to say it. The words burbled up from deep inside.

"I'm in love with you, too," she murmured.

"I know," he murmured back, but a large grin split his face.

"Why you…" She bashed his bicep with her fist. "What do you mean, you know? That's the first time I've ever said it."

"No, it's the first time you've ever admitted it. But I've known for a long time. I knew it was the reason you ran away the first time. Because you were too stubborn."

He tucked his arms inside her coat, wrapping them around her waist, pulling her closer. Words failed her, and she spluttered as she glared up at him.

"God, I love you so much," he said. "Especially when I render that feisty tongue of yours speechless." All the unsaid words died on her lips.

The world was a cataclysm around them, but Cat didn't care. All of a sudden, she needed Levi, and nothing else. He kissed her.

When they finally emerged for air, he said, "I know we can make this work, Cat."

"I want you, Levi. With your help, I can do this."

"So, you'll stay this time? For good?"

"Yes, I'll stay. But perhaps a little road trip isn't out of the question?" She quirked her lips up, lifting one eyebrow. Was it too early to test his resolve?

"You can't let a bike like that sit idle forever." His lips twitched as well.

"We could look into getting you a motorcycle. What do you think?"

"Only if it's bigger than yours."

"Now, hold on just one minute, Mr. Wilson."

"You know I was kidding," he said gently. And then he kissed her again, and all thoughts of motorcycles fled from her mind.

A thick plume of smoke drifted across their little oasis and Levi reluctantly let her lips go.

"I need to let Tom and Dean know we're still alive. As long as one of our phones still works." He frowned, and Cat came back to reality with a thump.

"Yes, they'll be freaking out." And they still needed to get out of here in one piece. They weren't safe, yet.

Levi had both phones in one hand, tucked around the back of her waist. He withdrew them, handed hers back, and thumbed his screen. It lit up, showing one bar of reception. They let out a simultaneous sigh of relief. She checked she too, had reception, then tucked it in her coat pocket.

While Levi made the call, Cat stomped around in their small patch of green grass, trying to warm up her lower body. She heard Dean's explosion of relief through Levi's phone, even though she was standing a few feet away, and her chest ballooned at the thought of how worried her boss must've been. Her sore arm throbbed, but not enough to worry Levi about. Later, when they were back at the cabin, she'd ask him to take another look at it.

"Tom got the newlyweds past the fire safely," Levi reported, as soon as he ended the call. "They're still on their way down, but out of danger now."

"Good." Cat drew in a deep breath and let it out. The news was a huge weight off her chest. She'd need to thank Tom when she got back to the ranch. If it hadn't been for him, they could've all died.

"And Dean's talking to the rescue services right now to organize a way out of here. They're going to call in the chopper."

"Cool." Cat had never been in a helicopter before. How ironic her first time would be as a search-and-rescue victim.

"We'll have to sit tight here for a while, though. It might take an hour or so, the chopper is still on its way back from Kootenia."

Cat shrugged. Normally, waiting in a scorched landscape, while she was cold and wet wouldn't have sat high on her list of fun things to do. But Levi was here with her.

"I'm sure we can find something to do to keep us warm while we wait," she said, taking a step toward him.

His eyes glowed with love and pleasure. "I'm sure we can."

CHAPTER TWENTY

"So, who lit those damned fires, then?" Levi glared at everyone seated around the kitchen table. They both wanted answers. Needed answers. It was late, probably close to midnight.

All the guests had eaten and gone back to their cabins, but he and Cat were still debriefing with the police. The newlyweds were so grateful to both Cat and Levi, thanking them so many times it'd become almost embarrassing, but even they had eventually headed off to bed. The rest of the staff refused to go, however. Sheriff Buchanan had said they could stay on one condition, that they kept their mouths shut. He wasn't going to have this turn into a free-for-all. Everyone was crowded into the kitchen; Gordon and Penny, Steph and Dale, Joseph and Stella, even Roxane and Janine, the two waitresses from town, had stayed to hear this. Dean and Naomi were there, of course. As were Tom and Emily, but Emily seemed to spend a lot of time whispering to Tom.

Cat squeezed his hand tighter. He hadn't let her go since they entered the kitchen, and he didn't give a damn if anyone cast them curious glances. She was his now. And he didn't care who knew about it.

Sheriff Buchanan shifted in his chair. "We don't have an

answer for that."

The hair on the back of Levi's neck bristled. He and Cat had been in the direct line of those fires, and they could've easily died. It was obvious Cat had been the target. Someone needed to stop whoever was doing this.

Deputy Jude Wilder grimaced at his supervisor's tone. The other deputy, Susan Nomad, also watched from her seat across the table.

"We've got the state marshal's office sending down the arson investigation team as we speak," Jude replied, before Sheriff Buchanan could say any more.

The forestry fire services were having a hard time containing the wildfire. Because it was in such an inaccessible place, and because it wasn't threatening any houses or communities at the moment, they'd decided to let it burn. A bulldozer had been brought in to cut a firebreak, to make sure the front nearest the ranch wouldn't cause the ranch a problem. At least the valley where the injured bear was hiding was lower down, and farther away from the fires. As long as he hadn't been scared off by the smoke, they'd still be able to go in and find him, as planned.

Levi had a quick chat with the forestry fire chief, Hector, after the helicopter dropped them back at the ranch. After putting out the flames at the edge of Dean's property, he'd come back past the lodge to inform everyone of the wildfire's progress. Hector was a good man; Levi had done a few fire safety training days with him over the past months. He trusted him. He'd had a couple of quick conversations over the sat phone with him already today, relaying locations and conditions. So, Levi listened with great interest as Hector agreed with Levi's first speculations; it did indeed look like the fire had been lit with a drip torch, or something similar.

Levi glanced over at Cat. She'd managed to wipe most of the soot off her face, but her hair was more grey than blonde.

They'd had time to quickly change out of their wet clothing, but that was all. The helicopter ride had been one for the books. Neither he nor Cat had ever been in a helicopter before, and there'd been a few hairy moments as the copter hovered, winching them in. But Levi had loved watching the sheer delight on Cat's face as they drew her up and then flew down the mountain low over the trees, giving them a great view. That was hours ago, and now all Levi wanted was a hot shower and a warm bed. Preferably with Cat by his side.

"It looks like Clayton may get bail," Hank added, with a glare in Jude's direction.

"What?" Levi's chair tipped over, he stood up so quickly.

"Settle down," the sheriff barked. "The fact is, Clayton was in jail when this wildfire was lit." The sheriff shrugged, as if that answered everything.

"But Clayton was at large when the first cabin was set alight," Levi almost choked, he was so livid. "Hell, we caught him the night the lodge was attacked. He was right here, on the property, remember?"

"Yes, we remember." Deputy Jude Wilder stepped in again, keeping the conversation calm. He and Levi couldn't really be called friends, but they knew each other. Levi often ran into him when he stopped for a quick drink at the Tin Can Bar. Jude was around his own age and Levi liked him, trusted him.

Cat stood as well, her beautiful face twisted with frustration. "So, perhaps he had an accomplice to light the wildfire. Perhaps he was still pulling the strings, even from inside lockup. You can't just let him go. What about the fact he tried to kidnap me? Surely, that's assault?" Hands on hips, she glared down at the sheriff. They'd had a quick conversation about Clayton while they waited for the helicopter, and Levi knew she still had doubts. But he was still their most likely suspect. They couldn't let him go until they were one-hundred percent sure.

Sheriff Hank pushed back his chair and stood. "Clayton has been charged with aggravated kidnapping, but that doesn't stop him from applying for bail," the sheriff said flatly. "I think we're finished here." He glared at Dean, who also stood, glancing nervously between Levi and the sheriff. Levi hadn't intended to piss off the lawman, but this was ridiculous. The police seemed no closer to solving the arson crimes than they'd been six months ago.

"Of course, we'll look into all the possibilities. As you know, we've cleared Mike Spencer, he has an alibi. And Mathew Davis is deceased," Jude said, also rising and picking up his cap off the table.

Levi sat up straighter. Narrowing the field of suspects was good. But not good enough.

As if Jude could read Levi's mind, he added, "But we're still checking into the other two people on Dean's list. Donald Garcia is living in Texas, just as Dean thought. As far as we can tell, he hasn't left the state in the past few months, but we're going over his movements with a fine-tooth comb, even as we speak. But he's no longer top of our suspect list." Deputy Wilder paused for a split second. "I'm not sure if Dean's told you, but he received another threatening email today."

"What?" He and Cat swiveled their heads simultaneously to stare at Dean.

"Sorry, I haven't had time to tell you." Dean looked like he'd aged ten years in one day. Between the fire and now the terrible email… The man was clearly worried sick.

Levi took a deep breath and reminded himself it wasn't just him and Cat caught up in this. Dean and Naomi had as much at stake as they did, if not more.

"It looks like this email is from the same person as the one seven months ago, back when this whole arson thing first started."

"You can fill them in on that after we've gone," the sheriff grunted at Dean, and turned to march through the door. "Deputy Wilder can keep you updated on anything new that comes to light," he called back over his shoulder. The two deputies followed Sheriff Hank, Jude giving Levi a grim smile, and Susan raising an eyebrow in Hank's direction.

"I'll see them out." Naomi scurried after the three cops.

Cat snorted and sat down heavily. "What's up his butt?"

Levi had to laugh. After all they'd been through today, Cat still had that feisty tongue.

"He's probably got a lot on his plate. I think he's got all kinds of questions being asked from higher up, about what the hell's going on down here." Dean sat back down at the table and Levi righted his chair and did the same.

"That doesn't excuse him," Cat replied, pursing her beautiful lips.

Tom cleared his throat. "If we're almost finished here, I'd like to go and grab a shower." He and Emily had remained quiet throughout the exchange with the sheriff. "Naomi already filled the rest of us in on the email this evening," he offered, by way of explanation.

"Sure. You guys need to go. It's been a really long day for everyone," Dean said, his gaze taking in all the staff still arrayed around the kitchen. He zeroed his attention back in on Tom. "I know I've already thanked you for everything you did today, but I can't say it enough. You went above and beyond, Tom. I'm eternally grateful." Dean stood up and offered his hand over the table.

Tom stood and shook it warmly. "Thanks boss. All in a day's work."

Emily slapped him on the back, and said, "Don't you dare make light of this. Dean's right, you did a very brave thing today."

Tom's face flushed, and he ducked his head. "Okay, okay," he agreed. "But even superheroes still need a shower." He held out an arm, indicating Emily go in front of him. "I'll make sure Emily is safe in her cabin, first."

"Thanks, Tom," Dean replied.

Levi watched as Emily disappeared down the hall to the back door, followed closely by Tom, who had his hand in the small of his back. Was there something going on between those two? Tom sure looked at Emily with longing. He'd have to ask Cat later on. He felt under the table until he found Cat's hand, and she twined his fingers through hers, sending a spike of heat all the way through him. They needed to get out of here and go somewhere private. Soon. His whole body ached to hold her, to make love to her. There was lots of shuffling and murmuring as everyone else turned to leave, and the three of them waited as the kitchen slowly cleared.

"Anyway, back to the email," Dean said, once they'd heard the back door slam shut. "Sheriff Buchanan had a specialized tech guy from the Missoula office look into it last year, and they came up with a few leads, but nothing solid. This time, however, they were ready for it, and they think they've managed to trace it back to the perpetrator."

"Who was it?" Both he and Cat moved to the edges of their seats.

Dean scowled. "Believe it or not, it's that old girlfriend of mine, Summer Donovan."

"Okay…" Even though Summer had been on the list, it still didn't make a lot of sense. Why was she threatening the ranch? What did she stand to gain from it? Was there a connection between the girlfriend and Clayton, perhaps?

"So, the police think she's holding a grudge? Even after all this time? That she could be dangerous?" Cat asked, a frown wrinkling her smooth forehead.

"Yes. Even though the email was supposed to be

anonymous, she went on and on about how I owed her and how she was going to find a way to extract that debt from me. She wasn't going to be ignored anymore. When she sent the first one last year, I didn't put two and two together. Her threats were pretty vague, like they could've come from just about anyone." Dean raked a hand through his hair. "But now we have a lead, I can see similarities between her emails and some of those early texts she sent me when we first broke up. I still don't have a clue what she's talking about, but the cops are taking it seriously. She's living in San Francisco, so I'm not sure how she could be doing all this from there, but who knows?" Dean shrugged. "I asked Daniella, my sister, if she could think of anything that might be bothering Summer; she knew her back when we were dating in college."

"What did she say?" Cat asked.

"That she'd always known Summer was a bit loopy, and she never understood what I saw in her," Dean said with a wry laugh, then sobered. "Just because the cops may have linked the threatening emails to her, it doesn't mean she's the arsonist. Her email's never mention anything about fires or arson. Nothing like that, they're only filled with vague threats, that's all. This might not even be related. It could be a terrible coincidence."

Dean was forever the optimist, Levi thought with a wry smile.

"But Stormcloud Station hasn't had any fires, or other strange goings-on?" Cat prompted.

"Nope." Dean let out a small sigh of relief. "Whoever is doing this seems to be targeting this ranch directly. The arsonist may not even know there's a connection between Stargazer and the cattle station over in Australia. I'm still keeping an eagle eye on Dale, though. He isn't taking this seriously enough." Dean scowled.

Levi hid a smile at Dean's protective tone as he talked

about his nephew. But he couldn't blame him. Dean had no children of his own, and Dale was the closest thing he had to a son.

"I'm just so sorry you got caught up in it all." Dean reached over and patted Cat's hand resting on the table.

"I'm a little worried that it's got something to do with me, and not you. I seem to be in the firing line—pardon the pun—a lot," Cat said flatly.

Dean looked up sharply. "I was a little worried about that, as well," he finally admitted. "But Sheriff Buchanan is advising that all the evidence points toward me or the ranch being the target. You're collateral damage, as they like to say. The arsonist is trying to get to me by preying on those close to me." Dean frowned and looked away, his jovial smile nowhere to be seen.

Levi didn't like to see Dean in such distress. It did give them insight into the arsonist, however. It probably meant whoever was doing this knew Dean better than most. Because they understood how deeply he cared for his staff, viewed them as part of his family, and would do just about anything not to see them hurt. Dean would've been less spooked if he'd been the direct victim of the arsonist than he was by having the people around him targeted, instead.

"You should both take care, though, to be on the safe side." Dean stood, his large frame towering over the kitchen table. "But you look like death warmed up. Why don't you go get some sleep, and we'll talk about this tomorrow?"

"Good idea." Cat didn't look happy at Dean's answers, but she tugged Levi's hand and tried to stifle a yawn behind her other.

"I'll walk you up to the cabin," he replied.

She lifted an eyebrow at his casual tone, but said nothing.

They said goodnight to Dean and walked out the back door into the cold night air.

"Stay with me tonight. I'll get Emily to bunk with someone else. We can jump into a nice, hot shower together." He couldn't see her face properly in the dark night, but the heat of her hand flooded him with desire. He couldn't think of a single better place to be.

He hesitated. "I really, really, really want to do that. But I also need to go home to feed Rekker." Blasted raccoon. He was almost tempted not to say anything. But his conscience would've intruded sooner or later, and then he wouldn't have been able to enjoy his time alone with Cat.

She stopped in her tracks. "Then I'll come with you. I'm not letting you out of my sight while there's a possible arsonist on the loose."

He burst out laughing. It was just so Cat, always having to play the tough guy. He grabbed her by the waist and pulled her into his chest. "I love you."

CHAPTER TWENTY-ONE

Cat fell into bed, all warm and steamy from the shower. And naked. Levi landed beside her and pulled the blankets up, so they were cocooned together in the dark. She'd found it impossible to keep her hands off him during their quick shower to remove all the smoke and soot. Even if he did keep asking her about her burned arm. But if he could manage restraint, so could she. He was right, though, this time she wanted it to be slow. They could take their time exploring each other; relearning all the best bits about each other's body.

She'd followed Levi's truck on her motorcycle back to his house. It was only a twenty-minute ride, but it felt like eternity, she was so exhausted. Rekker was fed and safely put into his enclosure for the night. A little unhappy at his perfunctory treatment, but at least with a full belly. Levi was still seething at the sheriff and his lack of answers. One thing was for sure, those fires had been intentionally lit, and neither of them would feel safe again until they knew who did it and why. But for tonight, Cat was happy to lie in his arms and forget about everything that'd happened today. There was plenty of time to go over all the permutations tomorrow.

Levi ran a hand lightly down her back, and she snuggled

into the crook of his arm. Her body remembered this place; remembered being with Levi. It was so familiar, and so right.

Why had she ever left him?

Perhaps she'd needed that time to re-think her life. To come to terms with who she was. It was hard enough working as a female mechanic, she had to fight tooth and nail to be recognized, to be an equal in the business, to gain men's trust. Cat had always used that as her justification for her brusque persona. To work in a man's world, you had to act like one. But after she met Levi, that justification didn't hold true anymore. He proved to her there were men out there who respected her for who she was; she didn't have to validate herself to him.

Thank God Levi had the grace to give her another chance. She wanted it to work this time. For both of them. If she let him, he would be her rock, her reason to stay every day. And she wasn't averse to spicing up his life a little, either. After all, life wasn't much fun if it was always the same old boring routine, day in, day out.

Dipping her head, she licked Levi's neck, just below the earlobe. He shivered, and she grinned. Yep, he was still ticklish there. She let her cheek brush against his beard and slowly found his lips. After only a few seconds, his mouth turned scorching and hungry, his tongue dipping in and out, turning her legs to jelly. Rolling over, she looped her legs over the top of his and flipped him on his back, laying on top. She gloried in the feel of his hardened muscles against her stomach, long thighs entwined with hers. Could you call a man beautiful? Well, she was going to call him beautiful. All that bronze skin, long, dark hair, and high cheekbones. But it was the person Levi was on the inside that was so attractive.

Slow and languorous be damned. She wanted him hot and ready for her right now. Which he was, if his pulsing erection digging into her hip bone was any indication.

"Just what do you think you're doing?" he asked, a slow smile spreading across his face.

"Taking what I want." She nipped his shoulder with sharp teeth. "You. You are what I want."

"I'm more than okay with that."

Their passion had always been strong and true. It'd been her inability to commit that'd been the thorn between them. Cat was now determined to beat that demon.

She wriggled against him seductively, and he groaned deep in his throat.

"Cat…" He didn't need to finish his sentence; she knew what he wanted. Moving up slightly, she let the tip of his penis hover at the edge of her core.

"Oh, you…" He clamped his lips shut tight and stared up at her, earth-colored eyes dark with passion.

She let him slide inside her and gave a groan of her own. They moved together, to a rhythm all of their own.

An hour later, they lay like two kittens, curled up together in the middle of Levi's bed. Cat sat up suddenly, as an idea occurred to her.

"Wait there." She hopped out of bed, goose bumps rising on her naked skin at the cold air after the warmth of Levi's bed.

"Where are you…?"

She ignored his surprised face peering over the top of the blankets. It only took a few moments before she was back in bed, pushing her cold feet up against his calves to warm them.

"Here." She took Levi's hand and pressed something into his palm.

"What's this?" Sitting up so he could examine what she'd given him, Levi turned the metal over in his hands.

"The keys to my motorcycle." She sat up as well, and pulled the covers with her, leaning her head on his shoulder.

"So you don't think I'm going to turn around and ride away from you again."

"Wow." He opened and closed his mouth, but no more words were forthcoming as he stared down at the silver keys in his hand.

"So you know I'll keep my promise," she continued, afraid he hadn't understood her gesture of good faith. The idea had come to her on a whim, as they lay snuggling. Had she done the wrong thing? "I'm here to stay, Levi."

"Thank you, Cat. This means more to me than you know."

He pulled her to him, and something fluttered wild and free in her chest. So, this was what it felt like to finally let someone into her world. To finally possess love. And give it in return.

* * *

Cat rolled over, not sure what had woken her. She snuggled farther into the warm cocoon of their bed. Hers and Levi's bed. The thought gave her goosebumps. Cat lifted her head off the pillow.

What was that sound?

There it was again. It was Rekker; he was growling almost like a dog and rattling around in his enclosure.

Nestling even closer to Levi, she ignored the little critter. But now she was awake, all kinds of thoughts were rolling around in her head, and she turned over to stare at the ceiling, listening to Levi's soft, regular breathing.

Rekker was still growling, his snarl getting louder in pitch. What was up with that animal? Finally, it was more than she could take, and she got out of bed and padded on bare feet over to the window to twitch aside the curtains and peer outside. The bedroom window faced the front yard, but everything looked fine out there, as far as she could tell. The street was illuminated by a weak new moon, but nothing… Wait a second…what was that orange glow? A faint yellowish gleam was reflecting off the far side of the house.

She grabbed Levi's T-shirt off the floor and, more urgently now, stalked out of the bedroom and down the hallway toward the living room at the back. When she pulled the curtains open wide, she gasped in anguish. Her bike. Her beautiful bike was on fire. The glossy black paint crackling and peeling before her very eyes, the front tire a smoking ring of flames. It was parked down the side of the house, right in front of the shed where Levi kept all his tools and other odds and ends.

What the hell?

"Levi," she shouted, racing for the door. "Levi, come quick." She yanked the back door open and started across the porch, throwing her instructions over her shoulder. "I need help. Someone's set my—" The rest of her words were lost as something hard hit her in the back of the head and everything went black.

What seemed like an eternity later, Cat groaned and tried to open her eyes, but found they wouldn't respond. Her head was throbbing so bad she thought she might throw up. Trying to lift her hand to her feel her head, she was momentarily dumfounded when her arm wouldn't comply. What the…? Her arms were tied behind her back and her feet were also tied together. Her eyes shot open at the realization. She was lying on the wooden floorboards on the back porch, near the back wall of the house. It was cold out here and she began to shiver. Then she remembered her motorcycle and swiveled her head around to try and locate it. It still smoking and fuming, but amazingly the flames had been put out. She stared at it in confusion. Why would someone set fire to her bike and then put it out again? And where was Levi? Rekker was going crazy in his enclosure up the back.

There was a noise from inside and a figure stepped out onto the porch, wearing a Stetson hat and a dark overcoat.

"Clayton?" she said groggily. "Is that you?" But that was ridiculous, because Clayton was in jail.

"Ha ha," a voice echoed out of the dimness. It didn't sound like Clayton. "That's great, my disguise fooled you, even close up."

"Who are you?" She demanded. "What do you want?" The figure came closer, removing the hat and staring down at her. It took a few seconds for her eyes to focus on the face in the dim moonlight. "Preston?" No, it couldn't be. He was harmless, and geeky…if perhaps a bit irritating. "You're the arsonist?" she said, not keeping the incredulity out of her voice. It was a mistake, because Preston scowled at her and rammed the hat back on his head.

"Why are you so surprised? Don't you think I'm capable? Well, you're about to find out how wrong you are." He gave a giggle and Cat felt a chill run down her spine for the first time that night. This guy was more than a little unhinged. It was all starting to make horrible sense. Pieces of the puzzle were clicking into place. Preston was the arsonist, and he'd been creeping around the ranch, right underneath everyone's noses.

"You got away from me up on that mountain, so I thought I'd come and finish the job," Preston said.

Shit, perhaps they should've been more vigilant. But no one had suggested they might be in danger again so quickly.

Instead of dwelling on that fact, she focussed on the here and now. "Where's Levi?" she demanded. "What have you done with him?"

"Let me show you," Preston replied, grabbing her under her armpits and hauling her backward over the hearth and into the living room. The room was dark, but light spilled in from the kitchen across the hallway. Who'd turned on that light? Was it Levi, when he came to see why she was yelling?

"There you go, together again." Preston dropped her in a

heap on the rug in the center of the room, right next to a warm body. Levi! Awkwardly, she turned over, the ropes restricting her movement, to find Levi unconscious on the floor beside her. Both his arms and legs were tied, as well. Preston must've hit Levi as he came out the back door, the same way he'd done to her.

Cat lifted her head and glared at Preston, the movement causing spikes of pain to shoot through her brain. That little prick. She was going to teach him a thing or two when she got free.

"What are you going to do with us?" she snarled, although she had a sneaking suspicion she already knew.

"I messed it up the first time. But this time, I'm gonna get it right." Cat understood Preston was talking about the first time he'd tried to set Levi's old house on fire. So, he could frame Clayton for the fires. Last time, she'd been there to rescue Levi. But who was going to rescue them now?

Cat knew the chances were slim to none of them escaping from this one, but she wanted to keep Preston talking for as long as possible. Perhaps an opportunity to get away might present itself. There was the small hope that someone had seen her bike burning and might come and investigate. She willed Levi to wake up, even prodded him with her toes, but there was no response. It was going to be up to her.

"You're not going to get away with this," she declared.

"Ha, why ever not?" He gave a small laugh and crouched down so his face came within a foot of hers. His eyes were black, endless pits, almost demonic in the dark below the brim of his hat, and Cat shivered. But she'd never been one to be cowed by any man. So, she pushed her chin forward and said, "Because it's only a matter of time before the police come knocking on your door. What's your plan when that happens, huh?" she taunted.

His lips stretched in a wide grin. What the hell did he have to smile about? "Clayton makes such a wonderful scapegoat. That's my plan."

"Yeah, well, there's one small flaw to that idea," Cat said smugly. "Clayton's in jail. The police will know he didn't do this."

"No, he ain't," Preston replied just as smugly. "Because he was released on bail an hour ago."

Uh, oh. Cat's heart sank.

"I'll make sure *Clayton* is seen leaving this place once it's well on fire. The police are so stupid, you can plant all kinds of supposed *clues* and those stupid assholes are none the wiser. I'll make sure I do it all properly this time." He let out another unpleasant giggle.

"It's still not going to work." Cat tried to hide the shake in her voice, but failed. This guy was certifiably crazy, but if she didn't come up with a solution quick, she and Levi might end up dead. "You can't fool the police forever. They know Clayton didn't light the wildfire."

"Maybe. Maybe not. With you two dead, there'll be no one left to point the finger at me. I'm not sure the cops are smart enough to figure it out without their star witnesses."

Levi groaned next to her, and she gave a gasp of relief; he was finally waking up.

"Levi, are you okay?" she called out.

"Yes. You?" His voice was raspy, and she heard pain behind his words, but he was alive and now they had two heads to pit against Preston.

"Nice to have you join us," Preston said, kicking Levi's bare shin with his booted foot, and Levi growled something unintelligible back. "Now I have both of your full attention, we can get on with the real business at hand." He bent down and retrieved a small metal container, then began to splash a clear liquid around the couches and up the walls. Cat sucked in a breath and smelled gas fumes. Shit, he was really going to do this.

"Preston, wait," she said urgently, her thoughts swirling wildly. She needed to come up with something to keep him occupied. Keep him talking, then perhaps help may still come. She turned what little knowledge she had about Preston over in her head. All she really knew was that he was a mechanic—a fairly bad one if Dean was to be believed—and he seemed lacking in self-confidence, was hungry for praise. She knew nothing about his family or relationships... Wait a second, that might work.

Preston pulled a lighter out of his pocket and snapped it on and off with a nonchalant flick of his thumb, and she almost forgot what she'd been going to say.

"You can't do this to us. We have friends, family who will miss us." Well, that wasn't strictly true. Cat only had her father, and he was estranged. But... "Levi has a brother and a father who care very deeply for him." She wasn't sure if this was true, but Preston wasn't to know that. She'd heard it somewhere that you needed to appeal to a criminal's emotional side, make them see you as a real person, get them intimately involved.

"Yeah, that's right," Levi added, joining in her little game. "It'd destroy my dad if I died now. He's not well."

Preston stopped flicking the lighter and stared down at Levi. "Ain't you the lucky one. You've got a dad." She caught a glint of something manic in his eyes. "I never knew my dad. Never had a dad growing up. My mom did the best job she could. Boys need a father, you know." His words dripped with bitterness, his voice so low she almost couldn't hear it. "I never had one to teach me right from wrong. But now I've found him, he's going to learn what it's like to live without."

Cat was confused. What did he mean by, *now I found him*? And how was burning her and Levi alive going to teach anyone anything?

Preston's thumb flicked, and a flame sprang up from the lighter. "But none of that matters to you, does it? You're like all the rest of them. All bullies who think you're above someone like me. No one ever treated me right, with dignity." The flame disappeared for a second, then came back as he jerked his thumb again. If that flame got anywhere near the puddles of gas covering the floor, they were goners.

A strange scrabbling sound came from the back porch. Cat lifted her head to stare at the hall just as a black shape zipped through the doorway and attached itself to Preston's lower leg. It was Rekker, and he was mad as hell. A snarling, biting, scratching ball of pissed off fur.

"Ow! What the fuck?" Preston yelled. He turned and tried to shake the demon critter off his leg. Rekker growled and hung on tighter.

Levi must've seen his opportunity while Preston was distracted, because he lashed out with both of his bound feet, catching Preston right below the knees, taking his legs from under him, and sending him crashing to the floor. There was a sickening thud as Preston's head hit the side of the wooden coffee table.

The lighter fell harmlessly to the floor nearby.

There was complete silence for three full seconds. Preston neither moved nor made a sound; knocked out cold.

"Rekker to the rescue," Levi said with a grin.

"Yes," Cat agreed with an answering grin.

CHAPTER TWENTY-TWO

Levi watched the man dressed in overalls load Cat's bike up onto his truck. It was a write-off, burnt almost beyond recognition, a mere skeleton of the beautiful machine it'd once been. Cat stood at the end of the driveway scowling at the man and his truck, and he was sending her nervous glances in reply. Levi went down and draped an arm around her shoulders.

"You're going to frighten him away, if you're not careful," he said quietly. It wasn't this poor guy's fault her bike had been torched, but the way she was glaring at him, he wouldn't be surprised if the guy took off without the motorcycle.

"Sorry." Her shoulders dropped, and she turned her face into his neck for a second. "That's my baby, you know."

"I know," Levi soothed. She used to say she loved her bike more than anything else in the world. At least he now knew he beat the bike. He rubbed her back in a soothing motion. Thankfully, the motorcycle was the only thing damaged in Preston's late night arson spree. An image stuck in Levi's mind, of those few seconds where Preston had flicked the lighter on and off, on and off. For a fleeting second, time had stopped. Even his heart had stopped beating. He couldn't lose Cat, not now, not after everything they'd been through. Then Rekker had rushed at Preston. Honestly, that little critter thought he was the size of a bear, and just as ferocious.

Levi smiled to himself, as they watched the man finish loading the bike and give them a wave before he jumped into the truck and roared off down the street. At least the motorcycle was insured, but Cat had told him more than once this morning that it was irreplaceable, and she had no idea what she was going to do without it.

A vehicle drew up next to them in the street as the tow truck pulled away. The house had already been flooded with about a dozen firefighters and the arson investigation team. They'd all since left, but the sheriff and one of his deputies were still inside, taking care of the final details. Levi wasn't sure he wanted to talk to anyone else right now, he needed a cup of coffee, a leisurely breakfast and time to recover from their escapades.

Dean stepped out of the truck, his face lighting up with one of his childlike grins, and Levi put aside his uncharitable thoughts.

"I hear you're some lucky people," Dean called, as he came around and opened the door for Naomi. "Look, your house is still in one piece and you're both alive and unharmed." He could always rely on Dean to see the bright side of everything.

Levi had to admit, it could've been so much worse. If Preston had more time to come up with his spur-of-the-moment plan, things may well have ended very differently. It was true, they'd fared well. It was going to take them a while to get the stench of gasoline out of the living room. They'd already moved the sofas and the rug outside to air, but he wasn't sure that'd be enough to cleanse them. But Preston hadn't been able to light his little fire, and the house remained untouched.

"We just needed to come and make sure for ourselves that you're both okay," Naomi said, pulling Cat into a hug. For once, Cat graciously accepted the other woman's heartfelt tenderness, returning Naomi's hug with delight. "We feel somehow responsible for all of this," she added, without letting go of Cat. "You know, because the arsonist started at the ranch, and all."

"Glad to see you safe and sound." Dean extended his hand to Levi and was suddenly struck at how this man was perhaps a better father figure than his own dad had ever been.

"Come in and I'll make us some coffee," Levi suggested. He took Cat's hand and led them all around to the rear porch. But as Levi went to open the back door, Sheriff Buchanan appeared in the doorway.

"What news have you got, Sheriff?" Dean asked, greeting the lawman with a firm handshake.

"Good news. I have good news." The sheriff actually looked happy. It was the first time Levi had ever seen him smile. He rested a hand on his gun holster and stroked his chin, but the grin never left his face.

"I've just heard from Deputy Wilder, he's interviewing Preston right now, and it seems he's singing like the proverbial canary."

Levi didn't blame the sheriff for the smug look on his face. This would be a huge relief. He must've been under a lot of stress for the past seven months. Being unable to catch the arsonist terrorizing Stargazer Ranch would've been a big thorn in his side.

"And we've got some interesting new information." The sheriff's grin faded as he fixed Dean with his stare. "It seems that woman, your ex-girlfriend, the one who's been sending you emails, is involved, after all."

"You mean Summer Donovan?"

"Yes. Preston's claiming she's his mother. Said she put him up to all of this. Which, of course, we'll have to verify. I think it's true, though. But he's also claiming…" The sheriff hesitated, and Levi looked from the Sheriff to Dean and back again. "…that you're his father."

"What?" All the color drained out of Dean's face, his ever-present grin retreating.

Naomi gasped and covered her mouth, and the poor guy looked like he just been hit by a ten-ton truck.

"Perhaps you should all take a seat," The Sheriff suggested. They all sat at the small table, while he stood on the top step and puffed out his mustache.

"That can't be right. I don't have a son. I don't have any kids," Dean said at last, looking first at the sheriff and then at Naomi. "You have to believe me," he pleaded.

"It's okay. I believe you." Naomi patted his hand sympathetically.

The sheriff went on. "Well, Preston's claiming he's your bastard son. His mother told him so. But you never wanted to acknowledge him, even when he tried to contact you. He said he even begged you for a paternity test. Preston Simison isn't his real name, by the way. It's Alexander Donovan. He was using an alias. To make sure you didn't recognize him when he applied for the job on the ranch."

There was silence as everyone digested this news.

"He never asked for a paternity test," Dean muttered, still in a daze.

"So, all of this was just to get back at Dean?" Cat asked. "No one else was the target?"

"I guess so. He wanted to ruin Dean," the sheriff answered. "Take away his livelihood. Said he wanted him to feel what it was like to have nothing. To live like he and his mother had done for the past twenty years. Everyone else was just collateral damage."

"You mean, like when you thought I was a suspect?" Cat said, glowering at the sheriff. She and Sheriff Buchanan would never see eye to eye. "And last night. That was all just collateral damage?"

The sheriff glared back at Cat a few seconds, but to his benefit, he cleared his throat and said, "Yes. That time he set fire to Levi's house was solely so he could plant clues that pointed the finger at Clayton, to use him as his scapegoat. I think at first, Preston had an idea he was going to blackmail Dean. Start small fires to make Dean worry. That's what his mother wanted, the money she thought she was owed. But then Preston got the job as the ranch mechanic and stopped lighting fires as the risk of getting caught became too high. And also, because Clayton had disappeared, and he had no one to pin them on. I think part of him also hoped that Dean would see the real Preston. Perhaps recognize him as his true son. But when Dean refused to reply to his mother's emails, and then humiliated him by firing him, Preston decided he wanted to make him suffer, the way he'd been suffering. Take everything away from him. I think he was planning to set Stormcloud lodge on fire, but he wanted to get you both out of his way first."

"Thankfully, his plan failed," Levi growled. He put a protective hand over the top of Cat's.

"This young man has a lot to answer for," the sheriff replied. "We're still getting into the nitty-gritty of it, but it seems that he did indeed frame Clayton."

Levi raised his eyebrows at that. Poor Clayton. Innocent all along, yet none of them believed him. How must that have felt?

"Was it just a coincidence that Clayton returned to town around the same time Preston started lighting fires again? At the same time I came back?" Cat asked.

"No, it wasn't." The sheriff puffed out his mustache at the

accusing tone in Cat's voice. "Right from the start, Preston pretended to be Clayton's friend, warning him the cops were after him. Clayton got in touch with him on odd occasions, used Preston as his eyes and ears while he was on the run. When Preston mentioned Cat was returning, he hoped Clayton might take the bait. And encouraged him to come back and try and convince Cat to help him clear his name."

"Hmm." Cat narrowed her eyes at Sheriff Buchanan.

He went on, ignoring her glare. "Preston can be smart, manipulative and conniving. But he's also totally naïve, socially inept, and confused. He's very mixed up, and after he told us about his mother, I can see why. She manipulated him into doing her bidding." By the lift in the sheriff's shoulders, Levi could tell he felt a tiny bit sorry for Preston. Perhaps if they'd befriended him, instead of ignoring him…

"We need to organize a paternity test. As long as you agree," the sheriff continued, shooting Dean a glance.

"Of course. I don't have a problem with that." Dean drew in a deep breath and stood, finally recovering from the shock of Preston's accusation. Facing the sheriff, he said, "But I know he's not my son. Because I'm infertile. It's the reason Naomi and I never had children."

Levi and Cat exchanged a look. He'd often wondered why such a lovely couple, who had so much to give, never had children of their own. At least this was the ultimate answer to Preston's accusation. He was just a mixed-up, dangerous kid, with a cross to bear, and had directed his sights at Dean, because he was rich and charming. Two things Preston would never be.

EPILOGUE

The sun sat low on the horizon, as Levi and Cat took a seat on his back porch. It was going to be a beautiful sunset, and this was the best spot to watch it go down over the Bitterroot Mountains. Levi would never get tired of this view. Rekker pattered around the porch, chittering at them to get their attention. He was hungry, as always. Levi handed him a chunk of apple. That'd keep the raccoon quiet for a few minutes, at least.

"That didn't take as long as I thought it would." Cat raised her studded eyebrow at him, and he had to laugh.

"That's because you don't own any furniture," he said, still chuckling.

"That's not true." She cocked her head to the side and glared at him, her blonde fringe falling into her eyes.

"One side table and two chairs don't really count." He softened his reply with a squeeze to her knee, but she bristled anyway.

"What about all my clothes? And all those tools we stored in the shed? Don't they count as well?"

"Yes, they do. I was joking." He stroked her jeans-clad thigh, enjoying the feel of the firm muscles beneath. Imagining both her legs wrapped around him, just as they'd been last night. Her crystalline-blue gaze zeroed in as she narrowed her eyes. Then her face changed, and she gave him one of her special smiles, completely unaffected and open. The one she kept hidden behind her tough exterior most of the time, but when they did escape, they were wondrous to behold. Levi's heart kicked in his chest. He could still hardly believe this amazing woman was all his.

"Of course you are." Cat sat back in her chair and began gently rocking. "I did sometimes wonder why I hung on to these chairs all this time." She patted the arm of the chair. "But they fit in perfectly here. With a little TLC, they're going to look great."

The chairs and side table had belonged to her mother, and Cat had kept them in storage for years, her gypsy lifestyle never allowing her to stay too long in one place. Although Cat never admitted how much losing her mother when she'd been so young had really affected her, Levi knew they meant more to her than just about anything in this world. Except perhaps her bike. And him, of course. She was yet to replace her torched bike, so that left him at the top of the pile, for the next little while at least.

She'd had her few meagre belongings shipped over from a storage facility near Las Vegas and they'd arrived today, including the collection of tools she'd been accumulating in the hopes of one day opening her own auto shop. The tools were stored in the old shed out the back for now.

"We can go out and buy a new sofa set together. What do you think?" He'd been meaning to get rid of the two ratty armchairs in his living room for as long as he'd been in this rental, but never found the right time or motivation. And they'd never been able to remove of the smell of gasoline from the equally ratty sofa, either. Now he had the perfect excuse. Something they could buy together. So they could put a stamp of their life together as a couple on this house.

At least the past two weeks had been free of any disturbances and wildfires. It sounded like Clayton had himself a good lawyer, because even with the kidnapping charges hanging over his head, he remained out on bail. They were all waiting for the case of Cat's abduction to be finalized and a court date set, but Clayton would definitely spend some time behind bars, he wouldn't get away with trying to snatch Cat, even if his motives had been those of self-preservation, he'd gone about it completely the wrong way.

Meanwhile, the cops were carrying on their investigation regarding the arson attacks, and it looked like Preston was going to spend a long time rotting in jail. Summer Donovan had finally admitted to sending the emails to Dean, which meant she could be charged under the criminal threats code, and seeing as how this was considered a felony, she could possibly also spend time in prison.

Levi cleared his mind of Preston and everything else surrounding the fires. He relaxed back into the cane rocking chair with a sigh. This was the life. He'd always loved this valley and the surrounding country. And now everything was perfect, because Cat had moved in with him. It was only a month since she'd returned to Bitterroot Valley, but they decided not to fight it. When something was this good, and it was meant to be, then moving in together was the next logical step.

Actually, it was so logical they'd been too preoccupied in the bedroom to move any furniture or tools for most of the morning. Luckily, it was Saturday, and Levi had the whole weekend off, for a change. He hoped Sunday morning was going to be spent in much the same way. In bed, tangled in the sheets with his amazing woman. And now they had the luxury of time, perhaps they should explore having sex in all the rooms, one at a time, or all at once, if the mood took them.

Levi threw another bit of apple in the air, and Rekker

caught it in his deft little paws and brought it to his mouth with a purr of pleasure. Cat gave a low chuckle. She thought the raccoon was so cute when he did it. And Levi loved that something so small and simple could bring her such pleasure. Rekker deserved a little extra attention after the way he'd saved their lives. Levi threw him one more piece of fruit as a treat.

He couldn't wait to spend the rest of his life with the woman he loved. That thought tickled something in his memory, and he suddenly recalled his brother. Shit. He owed it to Cat to let her know.

"Before I forget, I meant to tell you, Wyatt gets out of jail in a few weeks."

"That's great news. I can't wait to meet him." Cat never even blinked as she spoke, and Levi had a sudden suspicion she already knew. How did she do that?

"I might offer him a room to stay when he first gets out. As long as that's okay with you?"

"Of course, it is." She gave him a cheeky smile. "If he's as nice as you, I can't wait to be surrounded by more good-looking Wilson men."

"Hmm." Levi wasn't sure he was happy with that, but how could he fault her, she'd just agreed to letting his jailbird brother come and stay with them?

He checked his watch. "We'd better go get ready, or we'll be late." They were both looking forward to the big cookout Dean was putting on tonight.

"Sure, I'll go get my boots."

Typical Cat. Levi didn't even need to ask, he knew she'd be going to the party wearing exactly what she'd had on all day. It was her trademark outfit—apart from when she rode her motorcycle and then it was black leathers—blue jeans and a slim-fit, white T-shirt. Which he thought she looked stunning in, so he'd never be one to disagree with her fashion sense.

The T-shirt showed off the tattoos running up both arms. She'd told him she was going to get another one, in honor of him. Perhaps an eagle, his totem animal, but she hadn't decided, yet. He used to think she used the tattoos as armor, her own personal *fuck you* to the world. Which was partly true, but now he also knew they showed the story of her life. And he was glad he was going to be a part of that story.

Levi stood and grabbed Rekker by the scruff of his neck. The little critter wasn't always keen to go back in his enclosure, but a nice dinner of fresh vegetables and egg was always a good enticement.

Levi was going to change his clothes, even if Cat didn't. He wanted to look presentable tonight. But Levi wasn't sure he'd be able to eat anything. His stomach was all tied in knots and he took a few deep breaths to calm the sudden butterflies. The surprise he had for Cat better go down well. He wasn't sure what he'd do if she rejected him. The idea didn't bear considering.

* * *

The cookout was being held to celebrate the first day of summer, as well as a thank you to the staff and the fire service guys and gals who'd helped put out the wildfire. Everyone was in a great mood when Cat and Levi arrived. Cat leaped out of the passenger door of Levi's truck, eager to get a plate of that delicious-smelling food.

"Go on, I'm going to have a quick chat with Dean." Levi waved her away.

The Stargazer Ranch lodge had a large, undercover area, directly beneath the wrap-around porch, designed for this kind of occasion, with an extra-big barbecue set up next to an outdoor kitchen.

Emily waved to Cat, and she veered toward her, giving the food table an envious glance as she passed by. It looked like Naomi had outdone herself tonight, there were bowls full of potato salad, slaw, fresh-baked buns, and a huge pile of ribs that was almost as tall as Cat.

People gathered in small groups to talk and eat. Joseph, the head chef, was with Gordon and Violet, and Cat overheard them talking about perhaps adding cooking lessons to the list of activities offered at the ranch.

Penny and Steph stood too close to Dean's nephew, Dale, and Cat had to laugh. He looked mighty uncomfortable at two pairs of eyes trained on him, both vying for his attention. They kept gushing over his Aussie accent, and talking about how they'd always wanted to visit Queensland.

There was a larger group gathered near the bonfire, all chatting and eating. Cat decided they must be some of the firefighters. She'd need to remember to go over and thank them later for their hard work. Would the helicopter pilot be here, too? If he was, she wanted to give him a special thank you. She still couldn't believe how cool and calm that guy had been, hovering over a wildfire, winching them up to safety, making it seem as easy as riding a bike. Which it definitely wasn't.

Cat walked over to Emily, who was bunched in next to Big Tom and Stella. They all held plates piled with food.

"Is all your stuff moved in?" Emily asked, bouncing on the balls of her feet. Everything was exciting to Emily, and some of her infectious happiness rubbed off on Cat. "What's it like? Living with Levi, I mean?"

"Nothing's really different." Cat tried to frown at Emily. Just because she'd moved in with a guy didn't mean anything would change. But Emily kept grinning at her like an idiot, and Cat soon confessed, "Well, okay, it's kinda cool."

"Come on, Em, leave Cat alone. You know she'll never admit in a million years how head-over-heels in love she is with Levi," Tom said.

"Hey!" Cat put her hands on her hips, and the other three

burst into peals of laughter.

"You're so easy to rile up." Tom patted her shoulder and went back to stuffing his face full of food.

Cat snorted. Then she pursed her lips at Tom. But couldn't seem to stay mad.

"Well, if you really want to know, we had sex in ev—"

"No! No more, please." Emily held up a hand, horror written across her face.

"I bet you're sorry you asked." Big Tom bumped Emily gently with his shoulder. The look on his face as he gazed down at Emily made Cat pause. Did Emily know how Tom felt about her?

But before she could drag her friend away to inquire, Levi called her name and beckoned her over.

"Cat, I wanted to ask you something."

He fidgeted with something in his pocket, and wouldn't quite meet her eyes. What was his problem? Dean and Naomi stood together next to the barbecue, watching them intently. She wanted to get a plate of food, and her stomach rumbled loudly in protest.

Levi got down on one knee in front of her.

All the air left her lungs. The world seemed to shift on its axis.

Was he doing what she thought he was doing?

Oh.

He had something in his hand, and then he held up a little box.

A light blue stone shone out of a simple silver band, nestled in a fold of velvet in the box.

"Catriona Lawson, will you marry me?"

Her tongue stuck to the roof of her mouth. A flutter of panic flittered through her stomach. He wanted to marry her? He wanted her to stay with him? For the rest of her life?

She stared down into his beautiful face. Earth-dark eyes

fixed on hers. And the panic faded.

Yes. She could do this.

Yes. She wanted to spend the rest of her life with this man.

"Yes." Her answer was simple and straightforward.

Levi surged upward to take her in his arms. "Really?" He sounded like he couldn't believe his ears.

"Really." She stood on tiptoe and kissed his full lips, got lost in his mouth for many heated seconds. It was just her and Levi; nothing else existed for those few seconds.

"Now, do I get the ring?"

"Yes. Of course." He fumbled and nearly dropped it, before sliding it on her finger. "It's the same color as your eyes. And I made sure it was practical, because I know you wouldn't wear anything too big or flashy, that might get ruined."

She turned around and found everyone watching them. They all erupted into loud applause, and she flinched. She'd been so caught up in the moment, she'd completely forgotten there were other people watching Levi's proposal.

Naomi rushed over. "We're so happy for you both." Naomi practically glowed with pride, like a mother might've done. If only her real mother could've been alive to see this. How would her father react? Perhaps she'd call Bryan and see if he could track him down for her. She'd have to think about it.

Dean came over and clapped Levi on the back. "Congratulations. You did a good thing." He beamed his classic smile at everyone.

Then everyone was clustering around them, giving them congratulations. Emily could hardly contain herself, she squealed in Cat's ear over and over.

It was quite some minutes before she could drag Levi off behind the cover of his truck in the parking lot, where she kissed him until she couldn't breathe.

"How did you know I was going to say yes?" she finally whispered when they came up for air.

"I didn't," he acknowledged. "But I hoped."

"Thank you for keeping the faith," she said happily. Their life together was only beginning.

If you liked Wildfire then you might like the other books in the
Stargazer Ranch Mystery Series.

Combustion - Prequel novella

Firelight - Book 2

Snowbound: A Christmas Novella Book 3

Snowfall - Book 4

Cloudburst - Book 5

Also by Suzanne Cass
NEW
Stormcloud Station Series
(A Stargazer Spinoff Series)
Small Town Romantic Suspense
Clear Skies
Starlit Skies
Crystal Skies

Stargazer Ranch Romance Series
Small Town Romantic Suspense
Combustion: Prequel Novella
Wildfire
Firelight
Snowbound: A Christmas Novella
Snowfall
Cloudburst

Island Bound Series
Mystery Romance (on an Island)
Books can be read as stand-alone
Bound by Truth
Bound by Silence
Bound by the Stars

Colors of the Earth Series
Small Town Romantic Suspense
Books can be read as stand-alone
Shadows in the Dust
Shadows in Deep Blue
Shadows of Red Earth

Romantic Suspense
Single Title
Island Redemption

Glass Clouds
Chasing Bullets

Love in the Mountains Novella Series
Small Town Short Romance
Novellas can be read as stand-alone
Rain on a Tin Roof
Lost and Found
Rescue his Heart

Please Leave a Review

The greatest gift you could ever give an author is to leave a review. You will be helping other people to discover this book and making a difference to me as an Independently Published Author. If you liked this book and want other people to read it too, please leave a review.

About the Author

Suzanne Cass is an Australian author who writes rural romance and romantic suspense abounding with passion and danger.

Her debut novel, Island Redemption, won the Romance Writers of Australia Emerald Award in 2016. Suzanne was also a finalist in the 2019 Romance Writers of Australia RUBY award.

She had always had a fascination with the tough resilience of people who live in our amazing red-dirt outback country. When not writing about the characters that inhabit her head, Suzanne can be found roaming the Perth beaches with her border collie, or encouraging from the sidelines as her two sons play sport.

Acknowledgements

Montana has always been a fascinating place to me. I've always loved the nickname Big Sky Country, it engenders sweeping images of a sky so blue that it never ends and I had to write about it. And so, the Stargazer Ranch Series was born. The luxury ranch is purely out of my imagination, but what a place it would be to visit, if it were real.

Cowboys have always held a special place in my heart, as well. (As you may already know from my Aussie rural suspense novels.) They're courageous, tough, sexy as hell, and I like mine with a gooey center that only the woman they love will ever truly see.

Wildfire is the first book in the series, with Firelight coming soon. And there are plans for many more after that. I hope you enjoy reading about the people who live on Stargazer Ranch as much as I'm enjoying writing about them. Levi and Cat are the first couple to grace the pages of this series, and they have a unique set of challenges to overcome.

Of course, this book wouldn't have been what it is today, without the help and guidance of my author tribe. Jillian and Rose are two other authors who have given me unending support and loving counsel on taking my books to a higher standard. Thank you from the bottom of my heart.

There is a team of people who I also couldn't do without, beta readers (big thanks to Rebecca) and my ARC team, who are essential to an Indie Author like me. Big thanks to my editor, Tanya Saari

To my husband, Gary and to my two beautiful boys (who are turning into gorgeous men) Thank you for your unconditional love.

I am so very grateful to all the readers who have bought and enjoyed my books and who will continue to do so. Writing for you is what keeps me happy and contented.